RIDING TALL

Tall man.

That was Ruth Dawkens' name for Ruff Justice when he joined the wagon train.

She called him that, and gave him one kiss and nothing more. Nothing except an unspoken promise of what would come when they were further from civilization, deeper into the wild country.

Now it was dark, and she was alone with him.

"Nice night for a walk," she said.

"Seems to be," said Ruff. "You in the mood for it?"

"Yes," she answered, a little breathlessly. "I am in the mood for it, tall man."

And as she stripped off her clothes to reveal her lush, already-arching body, so was he . . . a tall man who was taller than ever. . . .

Wild Westerns by Warren T. Longtree

*Price is $2.95 in Canada

RUFF JUSTICE #17

DRUM ROLL

by
Warren T. Longtree

A SIGNET BOOK
NEW AMERICAN LIBRARY

PUBLISHER'S NOTE

This novel is a work of fiction. Names, characters, places, and incidents either are the product of the author's imagination or are used fictitiously, and any resemblance to actual persons, living or dead, events, or locales is entirely coincidental.

NAL BOOKS ARE AVAILABLE AT QUANTITY DISCOUNTS WHEN USED TO PROMOTE PRODUCTS OR SERVICES. FOR INFORMATION PLEASE WRITE TO PREMIUM MARKETING DIVISION, NEW AMERICAN LIBRARY, 1633 BROADWAY, NEW YORK, NEW YORK 10019.

The first chapter of this book appeared in *High Vengeance*, the sixteenth volume of this series.

SIGNET TRADEMARK REG. U.S. PAT. OFF. AND FOREIGN COUNTRIES
REGISTERED TRADEMARK—MARCA REGISTRADA
HECHO EN CHICAGO, U.S.A.

SIGNET, SIGNET CLASSIC, MENTOR, PLUME, MERIDIAN AND NAL BOOKS are published by New American Library, 1633 Broadway, New York, New York 10019

First Printing, December, 1984

1 2 3 4 5 6 7 8 9

PRINTED IN THE UNITED STATES OF AMERICA

RUFF JUSTICE

He knew the West better than any man alive—a hostile, savage land rife with both violent outlaws and courageous adventurers. But Ruff Justice had a sixth sense that kept him breathing and saw his enemies dead. A scout for the U.S. Cavalry, he was paid to protect the public, and nobody was faster at sniffing out a killer, a crook, a con man—red or white, at close range or far. Anyone on the wrong side of the law would have to reckon with the menace of Ruff's murderously sharp stag-handled bowie knife, with his Colt pistol, and the Spencer rifle he cradled in his arms.

Ruff Justice, gentleman and frontier philosopher—good men respected him, bad men feared him, and women, good and bad, wanted him with all the wildness of the Old West.

1

The sergeant wore a black armband, and when he spoke to the jailer, his voice was very soft. Beyond the gray stone wall of the cell a muffled drumroll was played. It was muted and dry, like the death rattle in a man's throat.

"Bixby."

Sergeant Albertson unlocked the iron door and Bixby just glared at him. The ponderous man in the first sergeant's uniform stepped past Albertson, the jailer.

"Time to go," Sergeant Mack Pierce said. Bixby, in prison stripes, spat on the floor and deliberately looked away. Outside, the drum sounded again.

"You go to hell," Bixby said.

"I guess maybe one of us is. Get up, Bix. Don't make us carry you out. Be a man for a change."

That stung Bixby and he rose to his feet as if he would take a swing at the first sergeant, but Fort Lincoln's first shirt, despite his bulk and apparent obesity, was a lot of man. Three hundred pounds of man, and if it wasn't all muscle, it was all determination, everyone knew that. Even Private Harold Bixby.

"I guess I'll come along," Bixby said.

Mack Pierce nodded. He had no taste for this, even

with a bastard like Bixby, who had ridden down an Indian boy over on the reservation and then shot the boy's father for interfering.

Pierce didn't like executions all the same. He couldn't recall but one other at Fort Lincoln during his tenure, and now they had two within a month of one another.

"You doing all right, Billy?" Mack Pierce asked.

The other figure in the cell was sitting on the bare bunk, pressed against the wall, unmoving. He didn't answer Pierce.

Bixby turned back toward the kid and grinned maliciously. "I'll let 'em know you're comin' when I get there," the soldier said. And then he laughed, long and harshly—until the drumroll sounded again. Then he was silent, he wasn't man enough for that.

Mack Pierce bent over and touched the younger prisoner on the shoulder. There was no response at all. Pierce patted the shoulder and then turned, walking out into the corridor where the guards waited to escort Harold Bixby to the parade ground, where he would face the firing squad.

The iron door clanged shut. Billy Sondberg lifted his head as he heard it. He saw the men shuffle off down the corridor, toward the outside door of the jailhouse. Beyond the stockade wall the drumroll sounded again and a sob rose up in Billy Sondberg's throat, pressing hot tears from his eyes.

It was a long while before anything happened. Billy sat stiffly, hands clenched together, head up, eyes alert although he could see nothing of what was happening outside.

When the volley sounded, Sondberg felt he had taken the shot. He let out his breath sharply as if someone had driven a fist into his solar plexus, and then he simply slumped over, his shoulder knocking against the cold stone wall.

He lay there, staring at nothing, watching the shadows

move across the wall of the cell. There was no way out, just none. There was no refuge. Only in sleep, perhaps. If he could sleep—just close his eyes and drift away from reality, from cold, murderous reality. And so he closed his eyes, but sleep was a long, long time in coming.

He awoke before he was ready to, but then it is difficult to stay asleep when someone is tickling you, running her lips along the inside of your thigh, when a mass of red-gold hair is falling across your abdomen and groin.

"Don't you ever sleep, woman?" Ruff Justice asked, and the face of the girl came up to smile at him. She crawled forward, catlike, her full breasts swaying. She gave a contented little sigh and snuggled down on top of the scout.

"I thought you'd wake up."

"And if I hadn't?"

"I would have continued anyway."

"Like that, is it?" he asked, wiping back the hair from her eyes.

"It is this morning, Ruffin."

He kissed her parted lips, then placed his hand behind her neck and kissed her again, harder.

"You wake up fast," she murmured. Her hand slid across Ruff's thigh to his very rapidly awakening groin. She leaned toward him, kissed his throat, and then sat up, quickly straddling him, lifting her body, positioning Ruff, and sliding onto him with a sharp sigh.

"You don't let a man catch his breath, woman."

"I've never noticed you running out of breath . . . or ambition." She swayed forward and then back, lifting Ruff's hands to place them on her full, nearly round breasts, where rosebud nipples stood tautly out.

She smiled very deeply, a sensuous, satisfied smile, and looked down into the face of the tall, lean man

9

with the dark mustache, the dark hair that curled down past his shoulders. His nose was nearly straight, but the bridge showed a slight curve, as if it had been broken once. It had. His mouth was thin, always faintly amused, sometimes cynical. The eyes were ice-cold, blue, knowing, but again the amusement was there. Life had been a grand game to Ruffin T. Justice, but he was aware of the final cosmic joke, his own mortality.

There were scars on his torso, arms, and shoulders. He was a warrior despite the fact that he wrote and read poetry, that he had traveled to Europe with Bill Cody and been entertained by ladies of various courts, that he knew wines—but did not drink them—in a country where raw whiskey and green beer were the rule. There were men who didn't like Ruff Justice, a few that were waiting to meet him again, to have another chance at killing him.

And there were a lot of women waiting to meet him again . . . for entirely different reasons.

All of his Corrine knew or read in the eyes of the tall man. Just now she was too busy *feeling* to think. She lifted herself and then slowly settled, her fingers dropping to her crotch to explore herself, to touch Ruff Justice entering her, and she shuddered again.

Ruff lay back watching the morning sun in her copper hair, seeing the concentration on her face, the pleasure behind her sea-green eyes.

Corrine was a giving woman, but when she needed to have sex, she took. She worked herself against Ruff, her pelvis gently thumping his, her distant eyes half-closed now as the muscles within her altered and loosened and the warmth began to leak from her.

"Ruff . . . damn you, don't hold back," she panted.

He had never wanted to deprive a lady and he didn't start now. Ruff drew her to him and rolled her onto her side. Her right leg lifted and then hooked around him as Ruff arched his back and drove his need home time and again, Corrine's fingers running across his lips, down his back, and to his erect shaft as she kissed his hard-muscled chest, his shoulders.

She swayed and pitched against him, cresting a wave of joy as Ruff searched her, striking home again and again, lighting Corrine's eyes, bringing her sensitive flesh, her bundles of overexcited nerve endings to a rushing climax. Ruff held her close to him, his hands clenching her smooth, firm buttocks, letting his own body find its completion.

She breathed in tiny little puffs, stroking his hair, kissing him lightly everywhere her lips could reach as her body spasmed and relaxed.

"Now," she said, "you can sleep."

"Now," he said, "I can't." He began to nudge her, to roll her onto her back, lifting her legs as his lips searched her breasts and throat.

"I want to eat, Ruff. A bath and then breakfast, all right?" She had her arms around his neck. She smiled as he plunged deeper into her body. "Oh, hell . . ." she murmured. "No one's that hungry."

There was a knock at the door and Ruff Justice managed to ignore it completely. He was on his knees now, Corrine's heels slung across his shoulders as he drove into her time and again, and her body—sweet, warm, once sated—began to come to life again. His fingers went to her crotch and he gently stroked her, spreading her as he sank into her. Her fingers joined his and intertwined, feeling her own dampness.

The knock sounded again at the door and someone softly called, "Mister Justice."

"Go away," Justice growled, and his hands slid beneath Corrine's soft ass, lifting her higher as he swayed against her, seeing her face lost beyond the mounds of her smooth white breasts relax with deep pleasure as he climaxed again, Corrine's fingers holding his shaft as he did, encouraging him, demanding more.

Her legs were straight in the air now, spread wide as Ruff again began a slow circular motion, his hands massaging the firm flesh of her breasts.

"Mister Justice!" The voice from beyond the door was growing insistent. Knuckles rapped on wood.

"I always thought this was a respectable hotel," Ruff growled.

Corrine laughed. "Better answer it."

"No."

"It may be important."

"I know it is. Anyone that would come around to disturb me while I'm off duty would have to have an important reason."

"Then?" She touched her fingers to his lips and smiled.

"Don't blame me if you never see me again," Justice grumbled, rolling away from her. "Just a minute!" he shouted at the door. Stepping into his pants, he crossed the room, sweeping back his hair. The hotel clerk in the hallway looked a little nervous, reflecting what he saw in Ruff's eyes.

"The man said to give this to you."

"What man?"

"A soldier." The clerk shrugged. He hesitated as if he actually expected a tip. Ruff closed the door in his face.

Corrine tittered. "Now, now," she said.

Ruff grunted a reply, walked to the window, and opened the note, reading it twice quickly.

He sighed and turned toward Corrine. "Is it important?" she asked, sitting up in bed, pulling a sheet up under her chin.

"Important enough," Ruff answered. The note wasn't real explicit. It was from Mack Pierce. Mack was asking a favor, and it was the only time Ruff could ever recall the big sergeant doing so. If Mack needed a favor, it was important. Pierce was the sort who took pride in

12

doing things himself. He ran that army post with a little help from Colonel MacEnroe.

Mack and Ruff had shared a canteen, a blanket, and a war or two. Justice looked at Corrine and shrugged. "Sorry."

"Oh, hell," she said with a short laugh, "you go on and do your soldiering. I'll be here when you get back."

Ruff dressed in buckskins. He fitted a new black hat over his carefully brushed hair, flipped his gun belt around his waist, picked up his sheathed Spencer .56 repeater and saddlebags, and turned back toward the bed.

"You need any money, Corrine?"

"Me? No. What for? I'll let you buy me breakfast, though."

"All right." Ruff left a little gold money on the bureau. She said she didn't need money, but Justice knew she did. That dress shop of hers had folded up flat. When he looked back toward the bed, she was lying there with her head on the pillow—and damn all if the woman wasn't sleeping!

Justice rode his bucksin gelding out toward Fort Lincoln. The Missouri flowed past, cold, silver-blue, swollen with upcountry rain. The fort itself seemed small and dark against the surrounding plains. There were more than the usual amount of civilians there when Ruff arrived.

He had forgotten—there had been a little amusement for them that morning. Harold Bixby. If ever a man had deserved to die, it was Bixby. But no man deserved to have his death, a very private matter, turned into a circus.

Ruff rode through the gates, feeling the subdued mood of the soldiers. He swung down at the orderly room, loosely hitched his buckskin horse, and walked inside, slapping the dust from himself.

Mack Pierce wasn't at his desk. That was unusual. The big man hated to move from his comfortable chair. Rising was a great effort for the first sergeant. Mack tended to remain at rest.

"What's up?" Justice asked the corporal of the guard.

"You want Mack, Mister Justice?" the kid replied. "He's in with the colonel."

"You want to tell them I'm here?"

"Go on in. They've been waiting a good hour for you."

Justice stepped into the colonel's office, surprised and puzzled by what he found there. Mack Pierce was drinking whiskey. The colonel was drinking it with him. An overstuffed, pleasant-appearing woman was watching them from the corner chair. All three looked around expectantly as Ruff Justice entered the room.

"You sent for me?"

"Yes. Come in, Ruff," Colonel MacEnroe answered. The old man looked worried. His silver mustache seemed to tug his mouth downward, His eyebrows were drawn together. "This is Mrs. Mary Sondberg," he said, gesturing to the woman, and Ruff bowed from the neck.

"How do you do."

The woman seemed unable to answer. Ruff could sense her grief, a grief so deep that perhaps she was afraid to try to speak, fearing the sobs that would emerge. Sergeant Mack Pierce moved toward her and the huge NCO stood protectively—and a little possessively—by her. A light slowly dawned in Ruff's mind. Damn the old cuss, he had a woman.

"Have we met?" Ruff asked.

"Mrs. Sondberg lives in Bismarck," Mack said, answering for her. "Justice has been away. Out in Colorado," Pierce explained to the woman. "He hasn't heard about . . . well, about things."

The colonel asked, "Would you like to go out and get a little air while we discuss matters, Mrs. Sondberg?"

"No, sir," she said, managing to speak rather firmly. "I would like to hear this. I've stood a lot, I reckon I can stand a little more. Please, Mister Justice, don't stand on my account."

Justice pulled up a chair and had a seat, balancing his hat on his knee as he sat waiting.

The colonel began it. "You know we had an execution this morning, Ruff. Damnable affairs. I don't like them."

"Yes, sir, heard about that down in town."

"Did you know we have another scheduled for next month?"

"No, I didn't. Who?"

"His name is Billy Sondberg." The woman choked off a little sob and Ruff's eyes flickered that way. "Yes, this is his mother."

"Desertion?" Ruff asked.

"Desertion!" That got the woman stirred up. "Billy would never desert the army. He loves it. Ever since he was a little boy and first saw Mack in his dress uniform— Sergeant Pierce," she amended, looking away briefly.

"I practically talked the kid into enlisting," Mack said, and his red, flaccid face looked tormented.

"No, you never did, Mack." The woman took his meaty hand briefly. "He always wanted to join."

"I used to go to visit on Sundays," Mack said to no one. "Mary would fry chicken and serve me lemonade. I'd sit on the porch glider, telling Billy tales about the Indians and all—most of 'em were true." He smiled crookedly.

"It's murder, Ruff," Colonel MacEnroe said quietly. "The kid has been found guilty of murdering a young settler woman. And unless you can find some proof that he didn't do it, he's going to face a firing squad on the fifteenth of next month."

The woman broke down then and wept openly. Mack

15

Pierce, looking awkward and weary, draped a huge arm over her shoulder. MacEnroe smothered a curse and turned sharply away as the tall man in buckskins sat listening, watching, wondering just what in hell they expected him to be able to do about it. And across the post a kid of eighteen sat in a dark stone cell counting out the last hours of his life.

2

The colonel took another slug of whiskey and sat glowering in his chair. It had gotten to him. Mack Pierce still hovered ineffectually around the woman, who looked ready to faint at any moment, but she was made of tougher stuff. She patted Mack's hand.

"We haven't given Mister Justice much information, have we?" She smiled, seemed to pull herself together, and sat up a little straighter. "Maybe we'd all better quit feeling sorry for Billy and for ourselves and start doing what we can to help him."

Mack looked at Ruff, smiled with a quiet pride and nodded. Colonel MacEnroe began telling the unhappy little tale of Private Billy Sondberg, condemned.

"We had a little trouble with some raiders down south, Ruff. I think it was that bunch of young braves Fox Fight led off the reservation."

"They haven't been rounded up yet?" Ruff asked in surprise.

"No. They've gotten a few new recruits, as a matter of fact. All these young reservation bucks are chafing at the bit. They want to get out and count coup like their fathers did. We lost a settler and his family down on the James River, had a minor incident out toward

Redrock—barn burned down, cattle slaughtered. Then at the end of last month Fox Fight started getting bolder. He tried a wagon train and had pretty good success with it."

"One Nate Stall was guiding," Mack Pierce put in. "Nate's been around a long while, and maybe he should have known, but no one was expecting a Sioux attack the other side of the James."

"Normally you wouldn't," Ruff agreed. The Sioux were all moving north and west, not toward Minnesota. But reservation Indians were a different story. When they jumped the fences, they generally did so with the idea of initiating a skirmish, of asking for trouble. They wouldn't run west but tended to raid in their own small, familiar area.

"Anyway, Nate didn't know that Fox Fight was in the area. He was running his show pretty loose, and when the reservation jumpers hit them, they hit them hard. Thirty-one people killed before they drove the Sioux off."

"I heard about that—all the way to Wyoming."

"People tend to hear bad news. It gets them stirred up," MacEnroe said with a grunt. "And you know where the blame falls."

Ruff did, and he also knew that fear of incidents like this was what got a lot of people—including people who should have known better—to thinking that the only real solution to the problem was the complete elimination of the Indian.

"We started picking up wagon trains at the James and escorting them through to Bismarck. That's the duty Billy Sondberg was on," the colonel told Ruff. The whiskey glass had somehow refilled itself. MacEnroe glanced at Mary Sondberg again. "Are you sure you wouldn't like to go out and get some air, Mrs. Sondberg?"

"No," she said firmly. "You go ahead, Colonel. I suppose if I've stood everything up to now, one more retelling isn't going to hurt me. Besides," she added emphatically, "it is all lies."

"All right. I sent out a patrol under Lieutenant Sharpe— you wouldn't know him, Ruff. He's down from Regiment in the last month. He's capable. It was nothing he couldn't handle—Fox Fight, most of the young bucks take off at the sight of blue uniforms, as you know."

"He has combat experience?" Ruff asked.

"Sharpe? Plenty. He was enlisted in the War Between the States. Battlefield commission at Chickamauga, confirmed later and made permanent by Sherman. Hasn't seen much of weapons since then. They'd shunted him off into Quartermaster."

"Just wondered," Ruff said. There was an enigmatic expression on the tall scout's face. "It doesn't have much to do with Sondberg's problem."

"No. Not much."

"What happened then? Murder, they called it?"

Mary Sondberg paled a little at the word and squeezed Pierce's hand solidly. The colonel nodded.

"Murder. Charged and convicted by court-martial—had three officers down from the adjutant's office, men with no grudge against the kid and no prejudice that I'm aware of. Guilty, they said."

"Who was it?"

"The daughter of a man named Maxwell. Sears Maxwell. A girl of seventeen. Raped and murdered. Sondberg was supposed to be on foot patrol around the camp, but when Lieutenant Sharpe went looking, he couldn't find him. Sharpe waited, sent out three men to look for him—for all they knew they had hostiles infiltrating—but no one could turn up Billy Sondberg. Until about midnight. The guard was changed. The man that was supposed to replace Sondberg found the kid in a hollow a quarter of a mile away from the night camp. The girl was there, dead. Sondberg was kneeling over her, in a daze."

"He didn't do it," Mary Sondberg said with a mother's conviction.

"Of course not," Mack Pierce said, looking at Ruff, who could only shrug.

"What did the kid say?" Justice asked.

"Nothing."

"Pardon me?"

"He said nothing at all. He was given a chance to explain, but he hadn't any explanation to offer for leaving his post, for being by the body, as to what had happened. He refused all through the court-martial to say a word in his own defense." MacEnroe smiled wryly, humorlessly. "It made things a little difficult for the defense counsel."

Something in the colonel's words grabbed at Ruff. He narrowed his eyes. "You, sir?"

"Yes. He asked for me; I tried to defend him. I didn't do a hell of a good job." The colonel finished the whiskey and jammed the bottle away in his desk drawer.

"I don't see what I can do here," Ruff said, shaking his head. "You expect Billy to open up to me?"

"I don't know what to expect," the colonel said unhappily. "You'll want to talk to him."

"A man facing execution will generally talk if he's innocent, sir. If he's guilty, he talks twice as much. What does it mean when a man sits quietly and waits to die?"

"You'll have to ask him yourself. I've tried without success to penetrate his reasoning."

"What do the people with the wagon train have to say?"

"To the army? Nothing. They came to the court-martial and sat there with blood in their eyes. They didn't have lynch ropes ready, but it was the next thing. I think it influenced the court-martial, I don't know."

"Of course it did," Mack Pierce said.

Ruff glanced at him. He couldn't recall ever having heard Pierce criticize an officer before. Mack was soldier through and through. This had really gotten to him.

"It's one reason I hoped you might have some luck, Ruff. These people trusted the army to get them through hostile country safely. Then one of them, a young woman, is attacked and murdered. There's a bitter irony there. I tried to talk to them before the court-martial and got nowhere at all. If they could have, they would have hung *me*."

"That bad?"

"Yes. That bad."

"What is it you want me to do, then, sir?"

"Whether these civilians want it or not, they're getting an army escort through to Bear Creek, which is where they plan on settling. I'm not going to let them get killed just because they think they have a grudge against anyone in cavalry blue.

"Neither do I expect any cooperation. I want you to guide this wagon train, Ruff. It's the only way we can hope to talk to some civilian who might have guilty knowledge. I can't hold them up at the fort any longer. They saw Sondberg convicted, now they're ready to go."

"You think someone saw something?"

"Someone had to. Unless . . ."

Unless Sondberg was actually guilty. It could be. "Could have been an Indian, sir," Ruff put in without much conviction.

"In that case we'll never know what happened, will we?"

"No."

"But I don't believe it was an Indian, and dammit, I refuse to accept the fact that this kid is guilty. He's a fine young man, Ruff. He was raised right." MacEnroe glanced at Mary Sondberg. "Someone with that wagon train thinks he's gotten away with murder. I can't hold them; I can't stay the execution. All I can do is hope that you can uncover something in time to save Sondberg's life."

Ruff's eyes met the colonel's. There wasn't much life in them. They both knew that this was an act of sheerest desperation. How was Ruff supposed to get the truth out of those settlers? As MacEnroe said, the guilty party had only to keep his mouth shut now. If there had been a witness to the crime, why hadn't he already come forward? How was Justice supposed to find out the truth, drag the guilty party back to the fort, keep the kid from getting stood up before that stone wall, tied to the old wooden post which was splintered from bullets, and getting himself executed?

"I want to talk to the kid," Ruff said.

"Sure. Want anyone to go along?"

Ruff shook his head, stood, took Mary Sondberg's hand briefly, and went out.

Mack Pierce waddled after him. "Ruff," he said, "thanks."

"I haven't done anything yet, Mack. Chances are I won't."

"I know. Thanks for trying."

There was anguish in Mack's eyes, anguish and guilt, which Ruff couldn't do a thing to assuage. He rested a hand briefly on Mack's big shoulder and went out, planting his hat on his head.

It was bright, cool. Beyond the front gate now Ruff could see several covered wagons. The settlers were preparing to move out. A mounted patrol rode past and Ruff waited for the dust to settle a little before crossing the parade ground to the stockade.

Sergeant Albertson looked up from his desk when Justice came in. He was a small-eyed, grim man whose job was making him grimmer. Still, he was one of these soldiers who figured he was suited better to a chair than to a saddle and he stuck to his stockade, apparently doing an adequate job.

"Hello, Mister Justice. Mack said you might be by." Albertson stood, hooked the key ring from its iron peg, and led the way down the dark, cool corridor. He opened the door to the cell and Ruff went in, hearing the door squeak shut behind him, letting his eyes adjust to the near-darkness.

The kid might have been carved out of wood. He sat unmoving on the end of the bare bunk, hands clasped, head hanging, lifeless. Ruff stepped nearer, but not too near. He was armed and the kid might feel desperate enough to take a long gamble.

"'Mornin', Sondberg." There was no answer. Ruff hunkered down, leaning his back against the rough, cold stone wall. "What did they do? Take away your manners when you checked in here?" Ruff asked. "Usually when someone says good mornin', a man answers."

Usually, Sondberg didn't answer.

"I saw your mother a few minutes ago."

The kid's head came up suddenly. A pair of haunted eyes turned toward Ruff Justice. "My mother," said a voice like a long unused iron door.

"That's right. You're a real bastard, you know that," Ruff Justice said with some heat.

"What are you talking about?"

"You know what I'm talking about. This deal you've handed your mother . . . or maybe you don't care what you do to her anyway, is that it, Sondberg?"

"I ought to . . ." He half-rose, his fists bunched, but the fire went out of him and he sagged back onto the bunk. "I love her," the kid said into his hands, "love my ma."

"Then why don't you let her off the hook? She thinks you're innocent. If you are, why don't you say something in your own defense? You kept quiet all through your

23

trial. You'll keep quiet until they shoot you. But you've got your mother fooled enough to believe you're innocent. You're letting her heart be torn out because you won't open your damned mouth to speak up and say what really happened out there."

The kid's mouth opened. He might have started to say something, but if he did, he never finished. He just wagged his head heavily as if it weighed a ton.

"If you're innocent, you owe it to her to defend yourself. If you're guilty, she ought to know that too. That would at least save her from false hopes, the despair of wanting to believe you, knowing she can't."

"I'm not guilty."

"Then talk, damn you!"

Ruff was on his feet. Abandoning caution, he stood over the kid and yanked his head up. "Yeah, you're guilty," Ruff Justice said.

"No." That was all Billy Sondberg said and all he would say for another half an hour as Justice tried pleading, needling, bullying, accusing. He wasn't guilty, but he wasn't going to do anything to save himself.

Justice went out of the stockade and found a narrow, dark-haired, green-eyed lieutenant with a scar across his tanned cheek waiting for him.

"Justice?" The officer slapped his folded gauntlets against his thigh.

"That's me," Ruff was forced to admit.

"I'm Lieutenant Ed Sharpe."

"Heard of you," Ruff said with a nod.

"The colonel says you're to guide the wagon train the rest of the way to Bear Creek."

"That's right."

They started walking across the parade. A small detail was moving out toward the main gate, riding in the back of a wagon. A buffalo-chip party, going out for the plentiful and hot burning fuel.

"I take it you had no luck with Sondberg," Sharpe said.

"Very little."

"I didn't think you would."

Ruff stopped. "You were with the wagon train. What do you think happened, Sharpe?"

"I wouldn't know," the officer said, looking away.

"You can't say anything that will hurt him now."

Sharpe looked toward the stockade and fingered the scar on his cheek. "No, I guess not. What I think is that the kid is guilty as sin. I think he got all stirred up by the Maxwell girl and did the deed, panicked after he raped her, and killed her to keep her quiet. Then, when he saw what he'd done, I think he went a little nuts. He was just sitting with the body when we found him."

"Why the silent routine?"

"A guess? Remorse." Sharpe shrugged. "He knows right from wrong, he just did wrong. Now he hates himself."

"Does everyone think like you?"

"Probably. Maybe not a few of Sondberg's friends. The civilians tell it that way."

They started walking again. Ruff was silent, thinking. At the orderly-room hitch rail he found his buckskin horse and tightened the cinches.

"What time are they planning on leaving?" Ruff asked.

"Three or so. They're in a hurry."

"To get to Bear Creek?"

"To get away from the army post."

"I take it your escort isn't welcome."

"Maxwell ordered us off. So did Updike."

"Updike, who's that?"

"Caleb Updike—he's the wagon master."

"I've never heard the name before." The two men walked toward the sutler's store, Ruff Justice leading the shuffling buckskin.

"Updike's not a professional wagon master, not a rough country man, I'd say. A storekeeper type, a big man, beefy, hard. He's got his secrets—I don't know what they are, but he's got them."

Ruff nodded absently. Everyone has secrets. He loosely tied the buckskin up and stepped up onto the plankwalk in front of the store.

"Who's been pointing this wagon train in the right direction? You? Or have they got a guide?"

"They've got one." Sharpe made a scowl appear vicious as he recollected something. "He's a mean son of a bitch, too. Mean and maybe a little too smart. He knows everything, or thinks he does, but he's reckless. He's a bad one . . ." Sharpe shut up as they entered the sutler's store.

A big-shouldered man in buckskin pants and red flannel shirt, torn flop hat, and mule-ear boots stood at the sutler's counter, licking a cigarette shut. Sharpe lifted his chin.

"That's him. Tandy Monroe."

Ruff didn't even hear him. When the officer glanced at Justice, he was shocked by what he saw. Ruff was leaning forward with animal intensity. His lip was drawn back from his upper teeth. The ice-blue eyes were hard and savage.

Tandy Monroe just froze where he was, his tongue still touching the cigarette paper, his eyes unmoving. Now he flung the cigarette away and took half a step toward Justice.

"Damn you," Tandy Monroe said, "didn't I tell you I'd kill you if we ever crossed paths again!"

3

The two scouts stood with their eyes locked, their expressions menacing. Ruff Justice handed Lieutenant Sharpe his Spencer repeating rifle and took a step toward Tandy Monroe. Behind the counter there was some activity—the sutler's name was Harry Grange; he hadn't been at Fort Lincoln long, but he had heard the stories. If Ruff Justice was on the prod, it was time to get the breakables down and put away.

"I said, didn't I warn you off my back trail, Justice?"

"Get out of here," Justice said through clenched teeth. "Get out of here and leave the door open on your way out so that some of your smell can drift out."

"Justice," Sharpe began, "I don't think that this is the time for—"

Neither man paid a bit of attention to the lieutenant. Tandy Monroe, who was a large man with a narrow waist, prematurely gray whiskers, and a sour-looking mouth, had put his rifle on the counter behind him and now he slowly came forward. Behind him Grange dropped a bottle of beer himself and it exploded. No one glanced that way.

"Goin' to use that knife, Justice?" Tandy asked.

"Shuck yours if you don't want to play that way,"

Ruff said, and Tandy, grinning, took his bowie from his belt sheath and casually flipped it across the room; it stuck quivering in the log wall. Ruff Justice took off his own belt, which held a big blue Colt revolver and his stag-handled bowie. He handed the belt to the lieutenant, who accepted it quietly and stepped back out of the way. If it was going to be fists and not guns, then Sharpe couldn't see any point in interfering. He didn't know what Justice and Monroe had against each other, but he did know that he would have given a month's pay to be able to put his own fist in Tandy Monroe's sour little face.

He must have gotten a little vicarious pleasure from the next few minutes, for the minute Ruff handed his gun and knife to Sharpe, Tandy Monroe stepped in, trying to get the first punch in from Ruff's blind side.

He wasn't quite quick enough. Justice saw it coming, stepped back, and countered with a left hand that went up over Tandy's wildly swung right and tagged cheekbone. Blood spurted from an inch-long, bone-deep cut on that cheek as Monroe, angry and surprised, stepped back.

"Damn you, Ruffin. This is the day you'll pay."

"Not unless I turn my back," Ruff jeered.

"You bastard," Tandy Monroe spat, making the word into a low growl.

Monroe kicked out with his right foot, but it didn't do much damage, grazing Ruff's thigh and going by. Tandy did better with his right hand the next time he threw it. Feinting to the belly with it, he swung a sharp left hook up and over, stinging Ruff's ear. The good right followed, catching Justice on the point of the chin, folding his knees a little, sending him staggering back, and Tandy Monroe yelled out joyously.

"Got you, you son of a bitchin', long-haired bastard, Indian-lovin' shit-eatin' dog!"

Tandy was as sophisticated as ever. He didn't quite

have Justice. As the guide moved in on Ruff, Justice, fighting off the effects of that one hard punch, managed to stab a left three times into Tandy's face. The nose started leaking blood and Monroe cursed again.

Ruff still felt unsteady, but his head was clearing. The hive of buzzing bees inside his skull was emptying out and he nearly had Tandy Monroe in focus as he blinked his eyes.

Having him in focus wasn't enough to fend him off.

"You gonna die," Tandy said. Then he leapt forward, throwing a wooden chair out of the way as Grange moaned in the background. The chair clattered to the floor and Tandy Monroe began windmilling punches at Justice, who had to back away, using his elbows to block some of the blows. Others he took on the chest and neck as he tucked his head in.

Tandy left himself open to a right and Justice sizzled one in. It caught the scout under the ear and he was knocked backward, stunned and astonished, to slam into the black iron stove that sat in the middle of its sandbox. When Tandy hit it, the black pipe that ran to the ceiling of the sutler's store folded and then came apart in sections, soot raining down as the pipe rang against the floor.

Soot-covered, bleeding from the nostrils and mouth, Tandy Monroe got to his feet. He yelled and bored in on Ruff, his head low, his arms going around Justice's waist.

Ruff was driven back. He came up against a counter with shocking force. The small of his back met the corner of the wooden counter and the whole twelve-foot section lifted precariously. The canteens, jeans, boxes of writing paper, sacks of dried fruit, tins of coffee that had crowded the counter were dumped onto the floor, and Grange yelled again.

Ruff went to the floor, Tandy Monroe on top of him.

Tandy threw a right that whizzed by Ruff's ear and struck the floor painfully, skinning his knuckles to the bone. A left had better direction. It caught Ruff on the cheek, spinning his head to one side.

"How'd you like that one, you bastard?" Tandy grunted. He didn't hear Ruff's muffled reply; he was too busying trying to drive his knee into Justice's groin.

Ruff got his hands free and put them in Tandy's face, tearing at his lips, nostrils, and eyes with stiffened fingers. Tandy yowled more with frustration than with pain, and fell back, coming to his feet to circle as Ruff Justice, up again, crouched, moved in with dark intent.

Ruff's own shoulders felt sore now, his arms heavy, both from holding them up and from the pounding they had taken. No matter, there was Tandy Monroe in front of him, and Tandy was going to take it. He had had a beating coming to him for a long time, and this time he was going to take it.

Ruff moved in close to Tandy; despite his longer reach, he felt more comfortable inside. His forehead nearly touched Monroe's shoulder as he held his head low and winged shots with either hand into Tandy's wind, occasionally going up and over to try for the shelf of the jaw.

Tandy wasn't backing up now. They stood toe to toe, moving in small tight circles, knocking over chairs or tables, leaving footprints in the soot, which was everywhere.

Ruff threw a right, grunted with the exertion, and then wound up with a left. Tandy tagged him on the heart and Ruff had a moment's confusion when his hands dropped, Tandy getting in a stiff jab before Ruff's head cleared and he went back inside, uppercutting to the liver and then to the chin. Tandy staggered back, colliding with a pickle barrel, going down in a sea of brine.

Ruff was aware of cheering and shouting behind him, of the crowd that had gathered, but he didn't pay them much attention until the too-familiar voice roared: "Break that up. With force if necessary, Sergeant!"

Ruff stepped back, panting. He glanced across his shoulder at the wreck of the sutler's store and Colonel MacEnroe, who had sicked Sergeant Ray Hardistein and six able soldiers on the two civilian scouts.

Tandy tried a last cheap shot as Ruff looked away. "You dirty bastard!" Monroe shouted, and the warning was enough to allow Ruff to lean his head away from the chopping blow.

Incensed, Ruff turned to counter, but Ray Hardistein and Corporal Reb Saunders had him by the arms. They were both good friends of Ruff Justice; but they were good soldiers first, and the colonel had told them to stop this fight.

"Easy, Mister Justice," Reb whispered.

Then there was no point in struggling. Other hands had taken hold of Tandy Monroe and he was being propelled toward the door, twisting, struggling, cursing.

"You are barred from this post, Monroe," the colonel said as the guide was half-carried past. The colonel's eyes were on Justice, however; perhaps he was tempted to bar Ruff as well.

And he had once.

Ruff shrugged away from the men holding him and stood there, breathing deeply, looking for his lost and trampled hat. The enlisted men who had rushed to watch the fight were being driven off. The colonel crossed the room.

"I don't even want to know what this is, Justice. Half the people in Dakota seem to be after your hide sometimes. What I want is the store cleaned up, the sutler paid, and you on the job."

Lieutenant Sharpe, who had been one of the more

enthusiastic spectators, now slipped Ruff his gun belt and stood by looking as stern as possible.

"I'm a little short on cash, sir," Ruff said.

"All right. I'll tell Mack to advance you some out of the company fund. How much, Mister Grange?"

While he and the colonel discussed the cost of the two-man riot, Ruff stared at the open door where Tandy Monroe had exited unceremoniously.

"Is it over?" Lieutenant Sharpe asked.

"No. Not with Tandy and me."

"There's the job, Justice. The kid. You'll have to put it aside for now. He's guiding that wagon train, or thinks he is. You're coming along. You can't help Billy Sondberg much if you're dead . . . or on trial for murder yourself."

Ruff wiped back his long dark hair, picked up his battered hat, formed it, and put it on his head. He didn't answer, but he didn't have to. Ed Sharpe knew as the colonel did that when Ruff Justice went out to do a job, by God he did it. Tandy would just have to wait.

But it wasn't over.

One of them would have to die before it was.

The wagon train was formed up outside of Fort Lincoln, the oxen hitched, the settlers—grim and severe—eager to be moving. The fort had a bad smell to them. They wanted to be away from it, away from the memory of the murder.

Ruff rode among them, looking for Caleb Updike. Updike, who was leading them onto the plains like a sort of western Moses. A man who, according to Ed Sharpe, had his secrets—whatever they might be. The man who had hired Tandy Monroe.

But then again maybe Updike didn't know about Tandy, know about the kind of drinker he was, about the party of Oregon-bound settlers Tandy had led into a blind canyon in a snowstorm over the objections of a man called Ruff Justice, who knew that area, knew they weren't going to survive up there.

"Updike?"

The man in the flannel shirt with the bushy red beard turned toward Ruff Justice. He had a folded piece of paper and the stub of a pencil in his hands.

"That's right. Who're you?"

"Scout. The colonel sent me out."

"I got a scout." Updike turned away.

"You got Tandy Monroe."

"That's right. So what? He got us here, didn't he?"

"Tandy must be running in luck if he did."

"What's up? You got a grudge against this scout of ours?" Updike walked over to Ruff's buckskin horse, tipped back his straw hat, and stood squinting up at Justice.

"I just happen to know Tandy some, that's all. Doesn't matter one way or the other how I feel, though. The colonel sent me to take you through to Bear Creek and I will."

"And I got nothing to say about it?" Updike asked a little hotly.

"I don't know about that either. They tell me to get to work and I do it, that's all."

"Who pays you?"

"The Army."

Updike shrugged. "Do as you please then. Can't hurt to have another man with us."

That was the welcome and the end of the conversation. Updike walked away again, calling after someone. Ruff looked around casually, wondering how he was expected to have any chance of finding the killer of the Maxwell girl . . . assuming they didn't already have him locked up. Ruff wasn't quite able to convince himself the kid was innocent.

There were seventeen wagons, maybe fifty or so people with the Updike party. Some, the kids and old women, Ruff could readily scratch from his list. That still left him with thirty suspects or so—and they were people he didn't know at all. Everyone would be occupied with traveling; there wouldn't be much time for talking to folks.

He removed his hat and wiped back his hair. A blond head poked out of the back of the covered wagon.

"Bring my stuff?" the woman asked. When Ruff turned his head, she saw she had made a mistake. "Sorry," she said. "I thought you were our scout."

"I am."

Justice was looking into a beautiful pair of remarkably deep-brown eyes. Blond and brown . . . he decided he liked it. The hair was softly waved, pulled back at the base of her skull. Her nose was slightly arched, the nostrils flaring, and her mouth was delicately molded with the under lip slightly full.

"Well?" she asked with a laugh.

"You'll do."

"For what?"

"Just about anything, it appears."

"I'm not used to men talking that way to me."

"If I've complimented you, I'm sorry," Justice said. She was still smiling. Her feelings weren't hurt much. "Tandy Monroe was doing some shopping for you?"

"Oh, he was going to the sutler's, so I asked him to get a couple of things, that's all."

"Are you a particular friend of his?" Ruff asked.

"Of Monroe's?" The laugh became a little harsher. "No. I can't say that. It was just convenient. Say, who are you to ask these questions, anyway? All I know about you is that you've got nerve."

"The name is Ruffin T. Justice." Ruff removed his hat again. "I'm going to guide the wagon train through to Bear Creek." He waited expectantly.

Finally she shrugged and told him. "I'm Ruth Dawkens."

"Mrs?"

"You are nosy, aren't you?"

"Interested, anyway."

She laughed again, shaking her head. "It's Miss Dawkens. I'm traveling with my sister. I'm twenty-four years old, and my hometown is Philadelphia." She asked pertly, "Anything else?"

"Not just now. We'll get around to it," Ruff said. He tugged his hat on, nodded, and kneed his horse forward.

The army escort was behind the wagon-train camp a good hundred yards. Apparently, Sharpe didn't want his blue soldiers any nearer the civilians than necessary.

"Got this solved yet?" Sharpe asked as he rode up.

"Don't I wish. I don't like the feel of this," Ruff murmured.

"You won't like the feel of this either: one of our Delaware scouts spotted Fox Fight twenty miles from the Little Missouri."

"Right in our line of travel. Was he sure?"

"He was sure. He knows Fox Fight personally from his reservation days."

"Just what we need," Ruff grumbled.

"I'd say so. Well, that's mostly my lookout. Yours is to do something for Billy Sondberg. Any idea how you're going to do that?"

"Not a clue, Sharpe. Not an idea in the world."

Ruff spoke to the soldiers before leaving. Only three or four of them were unknown to the scout. His room at the fort was adjacent to the enlisted men's barracks, and he had spent many a night with them singing, yarning, reading his poetry . . . whether they liked it or not. The NCO was Sergeant Lew Walters. Competent if not brilliant, a soldier doing his time. Walters played a decent mouth harp and was a terrible poker player.

"You hear about Fox Fight, Mister Justice?" Walters asked.

"I did. You don't expect him to tangle with a party of this size, do you, Lew?"

"I wouldn't, no," the sergeant answered, "but when the Delaware scout saw him, he swore that Fox Fight had up to a hundred men with him."

"A hundred?"

"Yeah—looks like his little army has built up some."

"Still, he won't want to tangle with yellow legs, Lew."

"You guarantee that, Mister Justice."

Ruff laughed. "They don't make that kind of guarantee."

Lew was still looking throughtful when Ruff left him. Justice didn't blame the sergeant. All soldiers have to expect to fight, but they can't be required to like it.

If Fox Fight had a hundred braves, it was puzzling and a little frightening. His band had begun as a few reservation jumpers. The warrior apparently had some good magic if he was continuing to draw followers. Ruff has guessed that Fox Fight would stay shy of the soldiers, but as he had said, there was no guarantee. It could be that Fox Fight would welcome the chance, wanting to show his strength and good magic against the enemy, thereby drawing even more recruits. You just never knew. Ruff would be riding wary.

He started out alone now. The first day's travel would be short and along a well-traveled road. They had no use for him. He took the buckskin out of the shadow of Fort Lincoln and rode it westward out onto the long plains, where it was still and empty, where Ruff Justice could just about smell the trouble ahead of him.

It wasn't going to be any picnic. He had the Indians out there, and back with the wagon train, a killer. There was a kid in the stockade due to be shot if Ruff didn't turn the trick, and an old grudge in the person of Tandy Monroe was riding over his shoulder.

There wasn't much pleasurable to think about as he rode on ahead of the wagon train, but he managed to find one thing to occupy his mind: blond and brown, *Miss* Ruth Dawkens.

4

The campfires glowed brightly against the night. Someone was playing a fiddle softly as Ruff Justice walked among the parked wagons.

He was looking for something, but he had no idea what it was. The only reasonable approach seemed to be to talk to as many people as possible. Very likely any conversation would eventually veer toward the tragedy of the Maxwell girl. It had to still be on all their minds.

Justice had seen Maxwell himself, but he hadn't had a chance to talk to him. Now he thought he had that opportunity. Maxwell was in the back of his wagon, struggling with a large object, cursing.

"Need some help?"

Sears Maxwell turned his dark, haunted-looking eyes on Ruff. "Pork barrel come loose," Maxwell said.

Ruff needed no more invitation. He climbed up into the wagon. He helped Maxwell shift the barrel and strap it to the wagonbed wall. It was only when Ruff straightened up that he saw the old woman.

Maybe she wasn't so old, but she was hollow. Dried up, empty of life. She sat on a flour sack staring at Ruff from out of the darkness.

"My wife," Maxwell muttered. "Since Katie . . ."

The old woman heard the name. "Katie came back? Katie came back? I knew she would, even when we buried her."

"Come on," Maxwell said to Ruff. The two men climbed out as the woman ranted on. Maxwell wiped his forehead with his sleeve. "Pork barrel weighs a ton. Don't know how it come loose. Do I know you?"

"Ruffin Justice. I'm helping with the scouting."

The two men shook hands. "Don't mind the old lady—she's not been right. My daughter . . . you heard about it?"

"Something at the fort. Guess they suspect a soldier."

"*Suspect!*" Maxwell roared. "Everyone knows damn well who did it. Court-martial found him guilty. He *was* guilty. I just regret we couldn't stay to watch him shot." The man quieted a little. "Doesn't bring her back, though."

"No, it doesn't."

Maxwell dipped some water out of the barrel on the side of the wagon and offered it to Ruff, who took a drink.

"Was this Sondberg your daughter's boyfriend or some such?" Ruff asked.

"Boyfriend? What do you mean? No. He was nothing to her, just another dirty soldier."

Ruff nodded with what might have been taken for agreement. "Going to farm in Bear Creek, are you?"

"Me?" Maxwell shook his head. "No, I'm prospecting. I've got me a little inside information."

"Hope you strike it. What about the boss here—this Caleb Updike. What's his game?"

"I wouldn't know, mister," Maxwell said firmly. "Maybe you ought to ask him."

"Maybe I will."

Maxwell perhaps was thinking that Ruff had been asking a lot of questions. He nodded a good night and went up into his wagon, where still the old woman sat maundering about her Katie.

Ruff turned and walked away.

It wasn't hard to find Ruth Dawkens' wagon and there she was, sitting on the tailgate, a lantern beside her, her blond hair down, doing a little sewing.

"I thought you'd be around," she said.

"Did you?" Ruff swung up onto the tailgate. "You were right, of course. How could I stay away from you?"

"Are you a sweet-talkin' man like the ones my mother warned me about?"

"If it will help, I'll talk sweet," Ruff said, and Ruth laughed again, deeply, heartily.

From inside the wagon a petulant voice rang out: "If you have to entertain your dirty men friends, why can't you go out on the prairie!"

"Shut up, Marcia."

"Your sister?" Ruff asked.

"Yes, worse luck." She spoke directly toward the wagon. "She's a pain in the neck! Old before her time."

"I am not. I just want a little sleep!" A blond head poked out of the wagon. "Is that so wrong to want a little rest after a hard day?" Marcia Dawkens demanded.

Ruff could see only her head. She held the canvas flap together around her neck, hiding her body. He was fascinated by what he saw, although it turned his stomach a little cold.

She had the same blond hair, the same brown eyes, but something had gone wrong. Nature had double-crossed Marcia Dawkens. Her right eye looked away from her left one. One seemed to be much larger than the other. Her nose, instead of being delicately arched as was Ruth's, was hooked dramatically. Her mouth was narrow and twisted. It was like looking at Ruth in an imperfect mirror, a bad portrait by a poor artist.

40

"Come on," Ruth said, "let's take a walk." Her voice was softer now.

"Anything to oblige. 'Evenin', miss," he said to Marcia, who made a small ambiguous noise and disappeared into the interior of the wagon. Ruff didn't say anything else to Ruth until they were well away from the wagon.

"Nice evening. Star bright and not too cool."

"I know," Ruth said obliquely.

"Know what?"

They stopped, facing each other in the darkness. They were well away from the camp now. The stars were nearly as bright as the low-burning fires.

"You're thinking about my sister," Ruth said, a little shame seeming to creep into her voice.

"Well, yes. It was a surprise," Justice said, choosing to be honest.

"I'm not a fool. I know that compared to her I'm good-looking. I don't know who it's harder on—her or me. She hates me, of course," Ruth added.

"I doubt that. Maybe a little jealousy. That's natural, isn't it? A beautiful woman like you." Ruff took the beautiful woman's hand and drew her a little nearer.

"It goes beyond that. It's one reason we're—It goes beyond that."

She looked down and Ruff tilted her chin up with a finger. "You have a serious problem with her?"

"I just don't know. Maybe when someone is too crooked outside things get sort of crooked inside, if you know what I mean."

Ruff did. "She seems nice enough, maybe a little tense. People get that way on these long trips."

"I think she's mad," Ruth said flat out. "I think she always has been. For years my parents took pains to be good to her, even to the point of snubbing me, lying to me about small things that happened. Now that my parents are gone . . ."

"What happened?"

"Why, the house burned down." Ruth was silent then. When she spoke, after a while, she had regained her high spirits. "Kiss me, sweet-talkin' man."

She didn't have to ask twice. Ruff folded her in his arms and let his lips roam hers, feeling the warm, soft press of her body against his. When she pulled away, she was a little breathless.

"That's all for now—my God, man, you are something."

"Let's walk on a way," Ruff suggested, and they did, arms around each other's waists. After a few minutes he reluctantly got to the questions.

"Ruth, did you know Katie Maxwell?"

"From one gruesome topic to the next. You're not so much fun as I thought."

"No? Want me to show you something?"

"Not tonight. Maybe . . ." She touched his cheek and turned away. "Yes, I knew her fairly well. In a small party like this with so few women, so much time together, you know everyone quickly."

"And Sondberg?"

She hesitated a little too long. "No. Not the soldier."

Ruff didn't press it, although he thought she was lying. "She didn't have a man—Katie Maxwell?"

"The soldier, I guess."

"Not according to Sears Maxwell or anyone else."

"Well, I'm wrong. I don't know. Why the deep interest?"

"Idle curiosity," Ruff said.

"Sure."

"Truth? I don't think he did it."

"Well, you're in a minority, aren't you?" she asked.

"I guess."

"I saw him around. He was a nice kid," Ruth commented.

"Meaning what?"

"Nothing. I still think he was guilty."

"Do you? Why?"

"The same reasons as everyone else. I mean, it looks like he was the only one with the chance. If he didn't do it, why doesn't he say something?"

Exactly. That continued to bother Ruff. He was silent for a minute.

"You know," Ruth said, "sometimes people don't like folks who ask too many questions."

"Is that so?"

"That's what they tell me."

"Is that the way you feel?" he asked.

"Me? Not me. I like you, tall man. How about one more kiss before you walk me back."

She got double what she asked for—Ruffin always felt himself to be a generous man.

It was too late to do any more poking around that evening by the time Ruff said good night to Ruth and left her at her wagon. The fires had been extinguished. No one was around but distant soldiers making their rounds, indistinct silhouettes against the starry sky.

He hadn't accomplished a thing with the night's work. Everyone thought Sondberg had killed the girl. Ruff rolled out his bed a good distance from the camp. His buckskin was cropping grass nearby, picketed there near Ruff.

Justice looked at the stars for a time, wondering. He closed his eyes and could clearly recall the worried, open face of Mary Sondberg, whose heart was breaking as her son stepped nearer eternity's gates. He could see Mack Pierce's despairing expression, the colonel's angry, impatient eyes. And beyond it all the shadowy figure of a murderer.

Justice's eyes came suddenly open. He rolled to one side as the pistol thundered out of the night. One minute Ruff was in his bed trying to sleep, the next he was scrambling from it, seeing the stabbing flame lift his blanket.

Ruff had rolled away from his own pistol and now he figured there was only one smart move. He dived at the ankles of his attacker, trying to knock him down before he could get a better idea of where Justice was in the darkness.

He heard a little *oof*, saw the ambusher fall. Then something hard clacked off Ruff's head and he swung out wildly, trying to lay his attacker low before he went out himself. They were suddenly under the horse, the buckskin rearing up in confusion, its feet cutting the air around them. Ruff rolled again to the side, his brain momentarily confused, uncertain, not able to choose between the horse's deadly hooves and the business end of the attacker's Colt.

He rolled clear, got to his feet, and made for his bed and his own weapon. His head still rang, his eyes refused to focus properly. By the time he found his Colt he was on his knees, alone, staring out at a silent night. No one from the wagon train seemed to be stirring. His attacker was gone.

Ruff got to his feet and slowly crossed to his horse, settling it. Nearly beneath the buckskin was an abandoned Colt. Justice picked it up and turned it over, but there didn't seem to be anything distinctive about it. He jammed it away behind his waistband and hunkered down to search for footprints. There was nothing to be seen on the hard ground, nothing clear.

He stood there, patting the buckskin's neck, looking down toward the two camps.

"Ask too many questions, did I?"

Already? He hadn't spoken to a handful of people, had accused no one.

"Maybe it was Tandy again." Maybe. Maybe it was someone Ruff had tipped his hand to unintentionally. Or a madman . . . or was it woman? It had been a long day with little rest. Ruff's mind still wasn't clear. In his head a strange dreamlike image formed itself. A woman with two faces, one beautiful, one twisted. She was the Dawkens sisters, but then her features would blur and alter and the faces would become those of an old woman, Mrs. Maxwell, who would laugh in his face.

Ruff decided the knock on the head had been harder than he had believed. He took deep slow breaths, clearing his head. In the morning the tracks might be more visible. The would-be killer might have dropped something. He would see. In the meantime he could only roll up in his smoldering blanket and try to sleep again. He didn't have a lot of success.

With the first gray light Ruff rolled out of bed, tied his roll onto his saddle, saddled the buckskin, and began his methodical search of the area. It was useless. Whoever it was had left no sign.

" 'Morning!"

Ruff looked up to see Ed Sharpe riding toward him. The sky behind the cavalry man was deep red and orange.

" 'Morning, Sharpe."

"What's up? Lose a collar button?"

"Something like that."

"Say, Tandy wants to make the Way Station Road—the old one. It seems to me the river bottom would be better. What do you think?"

Ruff looked down toward the wagons, squinting into the morning sun. "I'd be with you, Sharpe, but I don't think it's worth raising a ruckus over. It's just not that important."

"All right. I just wanted to tell you."

It looked for a moment as if there was something else Ed Sharpe wanted to tell him, but he never got around to doing it. He turned and rode out, leaving Ruff puzzled.

"I don't care for this game," he said to the horse. "I don't understand the rules."

Down in camp the oxen were hitched for the most part, standing patiently in their yokes, tails twitching, trying to graze. Weary-looking men and women, some of whom hadn't known how far this journey was taking them, clambered into the wagons or finished up the last chores.

Ruff rounded the back of a wagon, leading his horse. He nearly walked into a young dark-haired girl.

She let out a little squeak and dropped the water bucket she was carrying, staring at it then with dismay and something close to real fear.

"Sorry," Ruff said. "Did I frighten you?"

"I just . . . Thank you."

"My name's Ruff Justice." He touched his hat. The girl, who must have been all of seventeen, looked ready to bolt.

"Carrie Dean," she managed to stammer.

"Pleased. Want me to refill that bucket for you?"

"No, it's just . . ." She really was scared. Of what?

"Carrie!" the voice boomed from the far side of the wagon. When Ruff looked up a dark-haired man was staring into his eyes. He was scowling, his eyes cold and black as obsidian. He might have been an Indian except for his extremely pale skin, which now began to flush to deep red as he stepped toward Justice.

"Who are you?" Ruff told him who he was, but he wasn't listening. "What are you doing with my daughter?"

"Mister, I'm not doing a thing but trying to apologize for bumping into her. Neither is the girl doing anything."

"Carrie, get those water buckets filled! Do it now, girl!"

"Yes, Pa."

Carrie Dean scurried away, and her father, scowling more deeply still, watched her go. "You stay away," he told Ruff.

"Mister, I don't mind being warned off. Not if I was trying to do anything. But I'm not. I never saw your

46

daughter until a minute ago. She's too young for me, for another thing. You don't have to worry."

"I don't? How would you know. I know how women are. All of 'em are sluts. Every one. Even my wi—" He turned and stamped away through the mud the spilled water buckets had made, and Justice stood staring.

"Don't worry, Dean. I won't be spending any more time around you than I have to."

He shook his head in sorrow for the girl and led the buckskin to the Dawkens' wagon. Ruth had just finished latching the trace chains. Now she stood, dusted her gloved hands together, and blew a stream of breath up at an errant blond strand.

"Who's driving you?" Ruff asked.

"Huh?" Ruth turned with surprise. She smiled as she recognized Ruff. "I drive. Why?"

"I thought maybe you'd hired a man."

"You need a job?"

"I wouldn't mind riding with you for a time. If your sister wouldn't care." He lifted his chin toward the back of the wagon.

"She usually stays inside the wagon, day and night. I wouldn't mind a little relief on the driving—my hands are blistered. And I wouldn't mind a little company." She asked, "Do I have to pay for this?"

"Could be. We'll discuss that later."

He tied the buckskin on the back, feeling peering eyes on him as he did so. How mad, he wondered again, was Marcia Dawkens? That house that had burned down with her parents in it . . . the little hints Ruth had dropped—Ruff went back to the wagon box, climbed up, and took the reins from Ruth.

"Wasn't that Dan Dean I saw you in conversation with?" Ruth asked as Ruff nudged the oxen into motion and the wagon drew into line.

"It was a Mr. Dean, yes."

"Don't care much who you keep company with, do you?"

Ruff just looked at the girl, holding back a smile. "We weren't exactly friends at first sight." He told Ruth what had happened.

"Yes," she said after a thoughtful pause. "That sounds like Dan Dean. That poor girl of his."

"It must be tough."

"It is. She can't so much as look at a man."

"What happened? He blurted out something about his wife. She run off on him?"

"Yes, with some drummer man, they say—I can't say that I blame her. What sort of life could she have had living with a man like Dan Dean?"

"So he keeps his daughter tied down."

"Tied down . . ." Ruth's voice broke off as the wagon lurched forward. "Tied down? She can't speak to a man, look at one, mention one's name—and that's the truth. Not without getting a beating."

"You've seen him beat her?"

"No, not actually, but you feel it, you know. Watch that rock there, Justice."

"Want to drive?" He offered her the reins.

"God, no! I've been driving since Minneapolis. I'm fed up with it."

"Marcia won't spell you?"

"I told you, she won't come out. Especially not in daylight."

"It's really that bad?" Ruff asked in amazement.

"I'm afraid it is." Ruth looked momentarily dismal, but she shook it off; glancing at the bed of the wagon, she shrugged.

It was tough—and no place or time to talk about it. Jealousy or some more crooked, more dangerous emotion was eating away at Marcia Dawkens. She couldn't go out into the sunlight. She sat and watched and brooded, waiting for darkness. And what in hell did she do after dark?

The wagon train lined out toward the west and Ruff fell silent. There was much to think about, and not much of it was cheering. Ruth was quiet too, dozing off and on in the sun. On either side out a hundred yards or so Ruff could see the army escort riding, maintaining their distance.

Gloom had settled momentarily, but Ruff wasn't one for letting it take over. Glancing at Ruth, seeing that she was nearly asleep again, he leaned back and boomed out a song:

> I once knew a lady from Tangiers
> She wore diamond baubles on both ears
> Another was lodged in her belly
> But she only showed that one to sailors . . .

Ruth awoke, startled. Then, as Ruff broke into the second verse, she smiled, shaking her head. Ruff sang and the miles passed beneath the wagon. The cheer only lasted as long as the song. When Ruff closed his mouth, it seemed to come back: a knowledge that death was riding with them, that it had struck before and would strike again, and that there was nothing at all any of them could do about it.

5

They camped that night within two miles of Walker's Pass and the stage station there. Ruff Justice had helped to build that station for three enterprising young ladies who were still operating a stage line. After camp had been made, he drifted over to the stage stop, riding up just after sunset when a frail pink pennant still hung in the western skies above the far mountains.

Ruff was in luck. Dinner was on and Cash Williams, a troubleshooter for the line, was buying.

Buffalo stew was what they had. It was hot and good. So was the bread the Chinese cook had whipped up. There were a dozen or so people crammed into the small stage stop, waiting.

"What happened?" Ruff asked. "Have a breakdown?"

"You could say that. We've stopped running."

"Oh? Why so, Cash?"

"Fox Fight. We've got the end of our line cut off. The coaches stop here. My decision. No one's getting through to Bear Creek."

"That happens to be where I'm going. I've got a wagon train full of settlers."

"Uh-uh." Cash shook his head. "You'll never make it, Ruffin."

"We've got an army patrol."

"That won't matter. Up in those mountains cavalry's not worth a damn and you know it."

"Is that where he's holed up? The high mountains?"

"That's it, unless he's moved on. He got one of our coaches—it wasn't nice."

"Well, they're going to want to try it, I know that. The wagon boss is a man named Caleb Updike—"

"Updike!" Cash's eyes opened a little wider. "Did you say Caleb Updike?"

"I did. Why? You know him?"

"I know him. Ruff, he's a plain thief. Opened a bank in Leadville, stocked up the vault, and then cleared out, saying that the bank had gone broke loaning out big money to the mine owners to finance expensive equipment."

"Possible?"

"It was possible, I guess, but try telling that to a hundred rowdy miners who've just been taken for their gold." Cash shook his head. "That's all Bear Creek needs—a man like that."

"What qualifies him to be wagon master?" Ruff wondered, looking up as the Chinese cook poured him another cup of coffee.

"Same as usual, I suppose. A man has money enough to put the wagon train together and he elects himself boss. A lot of good people have died on the plains because of unskilled wagon bosses, people who paid their fee to a man who doesn't know any more about Indians or hard weather than they do."

"You sound bitter, Cash."

"I've got my reasons," the troubleshooter said. "I'll take them up with Caleb Updike one day maybe. He's not guiding this party himself—how'd he get this far? Your work?"

"Me and Tandy Monroe."

"Monroe! After ..." Cash actually sputtered with

anger. "I thought one of you two would be dead the next time you met."

"He's tried." Maybe more than once.

"Well, Ruffin, you've always been a man to take a chance, but I think you're riding with pretty bad odds now. If you try the mountains, I wouldn't give you any."

"No. I can't pull off, though. There's people depending on me."

"You want to do those people a favor, get them to turn back. Get them to get free of Caleb Updike too. I don't know what that fox is up to, but it'll be grief for someone at the end of the line, you can bet on that."

"Somebody mention Updike?" a strange voice asked, and Ruff, shifting on the chair, saw a tall dark man in black. The stranger had a toothpick in his mouth and a big Colt riding his hip.

"I did."

"I been looking for him," the stranger said.

Ruff looked him up and down, trying to place the man. A name wouldn't come. "Over east a couple of miles," Ruff said at last. "You'll see the fires."

"You riding back?" the stranger asked.

"Can't say when," Ruff answered. He didn't have any urge to ride far with this man.

"All right. Thanks. I'll get going. I didn't quite catch your name," he said.

"Justice."

"You're that one, are you?" The stranger's face was expressionless as he considered some private point. Then abruptly he turned and walked away, boot heels clacking on the floor of the stage stop.

Cash whistled under his breath and Ruff glanced at him. "I thought he was going to start something in here," Cash said. He looked toward the kitchen and Ruff saw the Chinese in the doorway, rifle in hands. Cash nodded and the cook withdrew.

"Is he supposed to be someone special?" Ruff asked.

"Some think so. That's Charity Blaine, the Colorado gunman," Cash told him.

The name and the face came together in Ruff's mind now. He had seen sketches of Blaine in the Colorado newspapers. There was some sort of apparently laughable murder case going on—in Leadville, was it? Ruff had had too much on his mind his last visit to Colorado to pay a lot of attention.

"What's he doing here? Why does he want Updike?"

"I'd like to think he was going to call him out," Cash said, "but the odds are he's been hired. They both hail from the same part of the country."

"Leadville."

"That's right. I think I heard talk that Blaine worked for Updike, but it's been a long while back. Ruff," Cash said, leaning across the table, "I don't envy you this trip you're taking. I don't get what's going on, but it looks funny from here. I'm glad I'm sitting this out."

"I wish I was," Ruff answered.

"You don't think Charity Blaine wants *you*?"

"No idea. All I know is that if he leaves first, I'll be riding slow and cautious; if he leaves after me, well, he'd best keep his distance. Something's up, damn me, but I don't have any better handle on it than you."

Cash walked him to the door. "You tangle with Fox Fight, and all the rest's going to become academic damn fast."

"He's gone bad, has he?"

"Real bad, and he's getting stronger. If we had time I'd tell you some stories that might even curl your long hair."

It sounded bad. The whole thing was a joke, a joke on Ruffin T. Justice and the kid sitting in a cell back in Fort Lincoln's stockade.

I'm not helping him a bit, Ruff thought. All I'm doing is getting myself tangled up with a bad lot. Tandy

Monroe, Updike, Dan Dean, now Charity Blaine. Ruff had no real reason for thinking Blaine was after him. All he did know was that Charity made his living in one way: gunning people.

Maybe the presence of the army would cool Blaine's murderous ardor. Ruff would have to talk to Lieutenant Sharpe about this new development.

Ruff sat his buckskin horse in the quiet of the dark stage stop yard. He could see the mountains stark and steep against the sky, the barriers they had to cross to guide the wagon train through. He slowly shook his head. He didn't feel up to this one, he just didn't. It seemed to be an exercise in futility all around.

When he rode out, he circled to the south before riding back toward the wagons—Charity Blaine had left first. He saw nothing, heard nothing but the mocking, stuttering bark of a coyote.

Or of someone imitating a coyote.

The gloom wouldn't lift from Ruff's shoulders this time, not for long minutes. Then he thought of something very nice and agreeable and he smiled as he lifted his horse into a canter, riding toward the wagons, where not only Charity Blaine and Tandy Monroe waited, but a very nice, very agreeable woman named Ruth Dawkens.

There she was on the tailgate of her wagon when Ruff finally arrived half an hour later.

"I thought you'd abandoned us," Ruth said, putting her sewing aside, hopping down.

"I just took a little ride. It was lonesome out there."

"Was it?"

Ruff has his hands on her waist, his mouth near to hers as he spoke. "Yes, it was."

"Nice night for a walk, isn't it?" Ruth said, looking skyward.

"It seems to be," he agreed. "Are you in the mood for it?"

54

"Yes," she answered a little breathily, "I am in the mood for it, tall man."

They walked together out onto the long grass plains. It had cooled a little. Distantly thunder rumbled. When they reached the low knoll to the east, Ruff kissed Ruth slowly, deeply, feeling the pulse in her throat with his lips. She rested her hands on his chest and then let her hands fall away to his crotch, where she touched the growing hardness and length of his shaft as Ruff kissed her again.

"Minute . . ." Ruth gasped, and she stepped back, performing dexterous magic with her skirts and blouse. Her skirt fell to the ground with her petticoats, making wreaths around her ankles. She stepped from them and returned to Ruff, who had taken off his shirt.

She was warm and soft in his arms. Her breasts, full, proud, were pressed against Ruff's hard-muscled chest. Her hair had fallen free of its pins and hung down across her shoulders in a softly scented, gently waving cascade.

"I'll make a bed," Ruth said.

Ruff made no objections, kicking off his boots and stripping off his trousers as Ruth spread her skirts across the ground. When Ruff came to her, she was on the ground on her back, watching him with hungry eyes. As he stood over her, her anxious fingers stretched out and encircled his shaft. Ruff could see the starlight in her eyes, the white glint of her teeth as a small, satisfied sound escaped her throat.

"Down here," she said, and Ruff obeyed.

Ruth rolled onto her belly and lifted her splendid white ass to Ruff's admiring eyes and hands. Her legs spread and her hand reached back, wriggling fingers urging Ruff Justice to move up behind her, to touch her warm flesh with his own eagerness.

"Come here, you bastard, and plunge in," Ruth said

in what was almost another voice. Her words were tight, breathy.

"In a hurry?" he asked. "Why?"

He was kissing her buttocks, the small of her back, easing forward now until his thighs were pressed to hers and Ruth's groping fingers found him and touched the head of his shaft to the warm inner flesh of her body.

"In," she panted, and in it went, sliding easily into her soft, damp cleft. Ruth quivered a little, her fingers still holding Ruff, still guiding him, touching him where he entered her, feeling their union.

Now her hand fell away and her head lifted as, on hands and knees, she began to sway back and forth. The night was still, the stars bright enough to reveal the intense concentration on Ruth's face as she rocked gently against him, her back arched, her strong supple body tense and alert as an acrobat's as she focused her thoughts, her being, on the small points of exquisite pleasure that Ruff Justice touched, stroked, tugged at.

"Again, more please," Ruth panted, and Ruff did it again, more, pitching against her, his hands clutching at her buttocks, spreading her, reaching beneath Ruth to grasp her breasts before with a tiny gasp she went to her belly, Ruff following her down, and he arched his back, slamming his body against hers, hearing another cry of surprise escape her body, feeling the satisfaction of her body flow across his thighs as he finished with a sudden hard, deeply satisfying rush.

They lay together panting, warm and naked in the tender night.

Her fingers ran across his lips, his eyebrows, down his cheek, her lips traveled across his throat and chest as she clung to him. The night cooled and their bodies stilled their pulsing. Reluctantly Ruff spoke.

"Maybe we'd better get you on back to your wagon."

"Not yet," she protested.

"What if your sister raises a fuss? Sends out a search party?"

"She wouldn't do that."

"No? I had the idea you never know much what she's going to do."

"Please, Ruff . . ."

But he was already rising. "I've got my reputation to think of," he teased. "Besides, there's always tomorrow night."

"All right." She sat up, defeated in the skirmish. She had her arms looped around her drawn-up knees and she watched as Ruffin dressed.

"You too," he encouraged.

"What's happening, Ruff?" Ruth asked suddenly.

"I don't quite get you."

"Yes you do. All these questions. They say someone tried to shoot you the other night."

"A jealous husband. Who said that, anyway?"

"Everyone." Ruth pulled her skirt up and shrugged. "You're not going to answer my question, are you?"

"Nope. Not now." He took her briefly and kissed her again, then let her go on with her dressing.

"Did someone really try?" she began.

"Likely it was an accident," Ruff lied.

Ruth didn't believe it much. "Tandy Monroe?" she suggested.

"Woman, I don't know. I'm all out of answers." He said it with some irritation, but he wasn't mad at Ruth. He was mad simply because he *didn't* have any answers.

Ruth caught his change in mood and she fell silent, finishing her dressing. When she was through, she gave him one last hug and they started down the grassy slope toward the wagons.

There were a few people still up, a handful more at the army camp, which, as always, was separated from the main camp. Ruff left Ruth at her wagon and started through the wagons.

Caleb Updike was at the tiny fire drinking coffee with a dollop of whiskey. So was Sears Maxwell and a few rough-looking men with tired eyes. Charity Blaine was nowhere to be seen. Maybe Updike was keeping him out of sight. Neither was Tandy Monroe around. Where the scout had been keeping himself, Ruff didn't know.

He told the wagon master and the others about the Indian trouble ahead.

"What do you want us to do, turn back?" Updike asked. He was a little drunk, so Ruff let the challenge in his voice slide past.

"Not at all. I would if it were me with my family and friends, but nothing I say is going to keep you people from trying to go through."

"That's right. We lost a lot of time at the fort waiting for the army to try that sniveling soldier boy."

"Yeah, right," Justice said, looking at the speaker, one of the hired hands trying to impress the boss. "I just brought it up because it's my job. If you vote to turn back, that's fine. If you want to go ahead, I suggest we ride wary. It's Fox Fight, they say."

"That Cheyenne reservation jumper! He's just a kid."

"Maybe. He's got a hundred other kids with him, though. And they've all got grown-up guns."

Updike had cooled a little. He nearly apologized to Ruff. "Didn't mean to flare up. It's been a long trail. Appreciate your information."

Ruff nodded and stood. "By the way, I ran into Charity Blaine. He show up yet?"

The smile that had been settling onto Updike's lips fell away suddenly. His words were icy as he asked, "What the hell are you talking about?"

"Talking about Charity Blaine," Ruff said as if with mild surprise. He couldn't quite read the bluff in Updike's eyes.

"Never heard of him."

"Funny," Ruff said before turning to walk away, "he said he was coming out here to meet you."

There was a dead silence at first and then, as Ruff got out of earshot, a few hurried questions, to which Updike growled short responses.

Well, he had served notice to Updike that he was ready if it was Ruff Justice Blaine had come to kill—

Except Ruff didn't quite believe it could be.

Updike had only set eyes on Ruff yesterday. How could he have hired Charity to kill Ruff? Not possible. Of course, it didn't mean that he couldn't be used for that job now that he was here.

"Where?" Ruff asked the darkness. He hadn't seen Blaine anywhere. It made no sense. He couldn't hide a horse. Even on the plains he would stand out to the night pickets—lyin'-down people on the other hand, are hard to see.

"'Evenin', Mister Justice," Reb Saunders called out as Ruff strolled into the army camp. The men there were at least a little more friendly. "You haven't been around much."

"No, I don't want to antagonize the other side."

"Antagonize away as far as I'm concerned," Reb said angrily. "I'd like to cut me off some of that civilian meat."

"It wouldn't be worth it. Trouble?"

"Just the usual crap."

"The lieutenant around?"

"No, he rode out a while ago—checking the sentries, I guess. He didn't tell me. Sergeant Walters is here. Asleep. I'll wake him, if you want."

"No, it's not that important. I don't know what he could do. No one's reported a civilian riding in, have they?" Ruff asked the Texas corporal.

"A civilian? No, sir, Mister Justice. No one's come in. The boys are kind of jumpy—you'd hear the challenge all the way to camp."

Then Blaine wasn't here. Where, then? He could have possibly slipped in and gone again. But that didn't seem to make sense.

Maybe.

Ruff told Reb about Fox Fight. "I'll report to the lieutenant when I see him, but it wouldn't hurt to pass the word as soon as possible to the men."

"It looks like a fight, then."

"Once we get into the hills."

"I don't favor that, Mister Justice." Reb had seen a few fights in the mountains. "A horse don't help you much. Indians know every crack and delve for miles and how to use 'em."

The corporal was suddenly grim. Justice didn't blame him. The idea of meeting a large force of hostiles in those mountains was distinctly unappealing. But Updike wasn't turning back and Sharpe's people would have to go along. They were in this together, like it or not.

Ruff Justice didn't like it much. He heard that lone distant coyote again and he glanced at Reb Saunders before looking to the dark, faraway mountains and shaking his head heavily.

6

They rolled out at dawn. Charity Blaine wasn't with them.

Ruff Justice knew that because with the first graying in the eastern skies he had dressed, saddled up, and without pausing to eat or boil coffee, had begun a diligent search of the camp and environs.

Charity Blaine wasn't to be found.

Down along a dry wash he found the prints of a horse that had been ridden up to near the camp, apparently tied for a time, and then ridden away, but the sand didn't take an impression well and it was an area frequented by the army pickets riding in and out of their rounds. Giving up on finding Blaine, Ruff had looked for Lieutenant Sharpe, who had also been missing last night.

"I guess you heard the word about the Indians," Ruff said as he rode up beside Sharpe on the left flank of the wagon train.

"I heard."

"Couldn't find you last night."

Sharpe smiled but his mouth was a little tight. "You must've looked in the wrong place. I was riding the

61

picket line once, letting the men see a touch of brass—can't have them getting too slack. Not now."

"Not now. You were at Chickamauga?" Ruff asked out of the clear blue.

"That's right." Was it Justice's imagination or did Sharpe grow a little defensive suddenly. "Why?"

"Just wondered. Enlisted, were you then?"

"Right again. How about you? You must have been in it."

"Sort of on the fringes," Ruff said evasively, although if the duty he had seen during the war was on the fringes, the vortex must have been hot, bloody hell.

"You're kind of getting carried away with yourself—these questions."

"Maybe. The colonel wants me to ask questions. A lot of them are probably dumb. Some," he said with an easy smile, "are just idle conversation."

"Sure." Sharpe smiled, seeming mollified, but his earlier irritation had been authentic enough. Ruff couldn't quite figure that out. Sensitive about having been enlisted? Perhaps there was something back in his war record that wasn't all so glorious as Sharpe would have liked. Justice wasn't out to dig into his past. He didn't care if Sharpe had been hiding in a hole through Chickamauga. What he wanted was the killer of Katie Maxwell, and he still wasn't sure if he was here or back in the Lincoln stockade.

And maybe, he thought, the killer and the rapist weren't the same person. He had eliminated women from the crime as a matter of course. Maybe, however, the sex act and the act of violence weren't related at all. Maybe . . . it was a world of maybes.

Ruff heeled his buckskin horse almost angrily and rose out onto the long grass plains, where the wind blew the scent of sun-warmed grass and the black-eyed Susans to his nostrils. His hair drifted back across his shoulders, and ahead, bulking large against the sky, were the Rockies, haunted by the living ghosts of the blood-ready Fox Fight.

There were five days left before they shot Billy Sondberg.

Ruff stayed well ahead of the wagon train, riding up the small canyons that met the larger gorge, Frenchman's Pass. He saw no Indian sign—maybe the Delaware scout had been wrong. Or perhaps Fox Fight had drifted out of the area.

There had been a lot of flash-flood activity in the hills and many of the canyons were rock-strewn. Only late in the day did Ruff find a promising trail.

It was airless in the canyon. Hot, dry, and the insects made a swarming mask around Ruff's face. The arrow sang past his ear and sent Ruff diving from the saddle, sprawling to the earth as the buckskin wildly galloped away. A flurry of motion, then nothing.

Ruff Justice lay behind a small clump of gray boulders up the lonesome canyon, peering upslope into the high sun. Nothing at all seemed to be moving up there, nothing alive on all of the mountain. He didn't feel like moving to find out if that was all illusion.

Ruff's sheathed Spencer .56 had gone flying when the horse took off, but he had the Colt .44 in his hand and some people said he was a fair shot with it.

But he didn't understand the situation. A wild shot by an inexperienced warrior, a young brave, a man alone? Why didn't he come on down? Most times pride alone would send a Cheyenne in to finish it if he thought he had his man.

This one didn't come. The shadows shifted; the sun slanted homeward toward the high mountains. The hum and buzz of the cicadas, and gnats, and the mosquitoes faded as the air turned purple and the shadows stretched out embracing arms from beneath the stack of boulders.

Ruff Justice heard the small creaking sound to his

right and his eyes shifted that way, darting at the shadows, trying to make out any movement among the patchwork of sunlight and shade.

He saw nothing, nothing at all. There was simply nothing there.

And then there was a blur of color and light, feathers and paint, motion and whispered sound as the Cheyenne leapt for Ruff Justice.

The warrior slammed into Ruff and both men sprawled against the ground, Ruff's Colt flying free, the breath torn from his body as he landed flat on his back against the sandy earth.

Ruff saw the knife arc through the air, but he managed to get his forearm up, and the Indian's downward driving arm met Ruff's wrist, blocking the blow. The Indian's lip was turned back in a savage grimace. Paint smeared his face, red and yellow paint, its once-intricate pattern destroyed by heat and battle. He had, Ruff noticed, only a single eye, and that eye glared malevolently as the Indian lifted his knife and again tried to bring the blade home into Ruff's flesh.

This one was a near thing. The blade was driven at Justice's face and only quick reflexes saved him. He rolled his head slightly, just enough for a miss, and the knife drove into the earth beside Ruff's head.

Ruff jammed stiffened fingers at the Cheyenne's eye, shoving his head back as he drove his knee up twice, three times trying desperately to drive the Cheyenne from his chest. The Indian grunted with pain as the knee landed on his tailbone. Off balance now from Ruff's attack, he was rolled to one side and the white scout scampered to his feet to face the Indian across the small clearing.

Ruff's hand had gone behind his belt and returned filled with his bowie. Late sunlight struck sparks on the dangerously sharp tip of the knife as he moved in, blade weaving, eyes alert, dark hair hanging in his face.

The Indian too circled. He was as grim as death, yet somewhere in the back of his mind Ruff would have bet the Cheyenne was enjoying this, enjoying the test of strength, the struggle for survival, the challenge that is life against death.

Ruff felt it himself. His blood sang in his ears. His throat was dry. The first man to make the wrong move would die. He who lost control of the bundles of nerves, the war-hardened muscles, the tensed sinews, would die.

"Is this a good time for it?" Ruff asked in the Cheyenne tongue. "Is this a good place to die?"

The Indian's eyes flickered slightly, with what emotion Ruff didn't know. Maybe it surprised him to hear his own language. Maybe it had unnerved him just a little, as Justice had hoped. Ruff wanted the Indian to think that he was not afraid, that he had fought many times, that he was no greenhorn, that he knew the ways of the plains, the language of the people of the plains.

The Cheyenne lunged and Ruff countered with his knife. Steel rang against steel and the Indian leapt back, his mouth twisting. The sun was lower yet. Only a spray of gold showed on the high peak, like a fire on the mountain.

The Cheyenne held his knife low, cutting edge up. He moved around Ruff Justice in a crouch, his knife darting out from time to time like a snake's tongue, watching, waiting patiently for an opening.

Ruff couldn't afford to wait. Did this one have friends nearby in the hills? The odds were he did. Ruff couldn't count on anyone showing up to help him. The shadows were very deep. The sun was gone completely.

The Indian continued to circle and now Ruff took the fight to him, liking the weight of the knife in his hands, the sureness of the muscles and brain that wielded it.

"Good-bye," Ruff said. "It was a good fight."

He feinted left and then cut right, and the Indian grunted with surprised pain. His free hand had been struck. A severed finger dangled from a bit of skin. Blood stained the earth and the Cheyenne's moccasin. It did nothing to frighten the Indian. He had come to fight. He had been struck, that was all—it was to be expected.

He came suddenly forward in a sort of crow hop, his head low, his rawhide-handled knife striking from side to side across the front of Ruff's shirt, slicing open the shirtfront and cutting a narrow gash in the flesh beneath. If Ruff had been any slower in leaping back, the game would have ended right there. The Cheyenne would have had the long hair to sing over and Ruff would have had what was always predicted for him—a shallow grave up a rocky, nameless canyon.

It didn't end that way. Ruff leapt back, and the Indian, suddenly overconfident or perhaps anxious because of the failing light, continued in. Ruff stuck out his foot and the Cheyenne went down over it. Before he could get up, Justice was on him like a big cat, mauling the Cheyenne.

There was no sound at all in the canyon for a time but the grunting exertions of men in combat, flesh against flesh, steel clicking off steel.

Then the big bowie rose again and the Cheyenne knew it was coming. His eyes flashed some message Ruff didn't get, his face twisted into a horrified mask. The blade of the bowie went in at the base of the Indian's throat and he thrashed against it, twisting and struggling for a last moment as he tried to strike out at Ruff, to tear the blade from his body. It was futile and Ruff just lay there, holding his bloody knife against the Indian's heated body.

He lay still, panting, the darkness sheathing them. Ruff just lay there, feeling the press of warmth against him. The life had gone out of the Indian now, dispatched by the magic steel. He lay there sleeping. Soon he would walk the Hanging Road with his fathers and hunt many buffalo in a land where the white men would never come.

Ruff rose shakily and tugged his knife free, wiping it clean on the Cheyenne's leggings. He tucked it away in its sheath, swept back his hair, and holding his wounded stomach, he staggered back to where he had lost his Colt.

Luck was with him. He found the pistol and the sheathed Spencer carbine. The horse was a different story.

"Deserter," Justice muttered. He peered at the cut on his abdomen, assuring himself it was only a near thing and nothing more, then began trudging off toward the mouth of the canyon and the plains beyond as an owl called distantly in the rocky foothills.

His buckskin had gone back to the wagon train. Ruth Dawkens had it when Justice finally reached the camp.

"My God, tall man," she said with what seemed to be genuine anger. "Where in hell have you been? I thought you were dead."

"No, but I was working on it."

"You're hurt—damn you, you're hurt."

"Not bad. Let me sit down, Ruth, will you? Damn that horse of mine, no man should have to walk that far in boots."

"Come on." She took his arm. "I'll help you to my wagon."

"It's nothing," he protested.

"We'll see that it stays that way," she told him, and there was no arguing with the woman. She led him along toward the wagon, the buckskin horse following like a shamed child.

"Just a minute," Ruth said, and she peered inside the wagon's drawn canvas. "Marcia! Are you decent?" She turned toward Ruff again with a frown. "She's not there . . . But she's always there."

"Nothing is always," Ruff said.

"No. Maybe she . . ." Ruth shrugged it off. Climbing inside the wagon, she got a box of bandages and a jar of salve. "It doesn't need sewing up, does it?"

"No," Ruff answered.

"Good. I hate that kind of work."

"No more than I'd hate having you do it," Ruff promised her.

She returned, ordered him to remove his shirt, and got to it.

Ruff watched her, smiling faintly, liking the deft touch of her fingers, the concentration on her face, the pursed lips.

"What's so funny?" she asked without looking up. She tied a knot in the bandage and bit it to start a tear.

"Not funny. Just pleasant," Ruff said.

"Yeah, we could have a lot of pleasant times," Ruth said, straightening up from her work. "You going out getting stabbed, shot, and clubbed, me bandaging you up."

Ruff laughed and drew her to him. She was on the ground and he was sitting on the tailgate of the wagon so he had to bend far down to kiss her. When he looked up, Marcia Dawkens was there watching, her twisted face dark with anger, her eyes glaring in the lamplight.

"Ruth," she shrieked, and Ruth turned toward her, the smile on her face falling away. "How dare you—how can you!"

"Now, Marcia. Please. Don't get yourself excited."

"Excited! Here you are acting like a common slut. I'm not to get excited?" She stood, her breasts heaving, staring at her sister and then Ruff Justice. "He hasn't even got a shirt on! If you don't mind, may I get into my own wagon?" she demanded harshly.

Ruff leapt down and let her by. When he stretched out a hand to help her up, she gave him a look that would have withered a rattlesnake.

Then she was up and gone. Ruth shrugged an apology. "It can't be helped."

"It's all right," Ruff said. He was taking a white cotton shirt from his saddlebags. Slipping into it, he could feel that he was going to have a little trouble dressing and undressing for a few days. He glanced at the wagon.

"I'd better let you settle down for the night. Thanks for the doctoring."

"You don't want to take a little walk?" she asked, lifting one hand to rest it on his chest.

"Not tonight, I guess." Ruff looked at the wagon. "Better not."

"You're right. Well, I'd better—"

From across the camp a man's loud roar and a crash interrupted Ruth Dawkens. Ruff glanced at her and then started sprinting toward the source of the noise, thinking first of Indian trouble.

It wasn't.

Ruff rounded the last wagon in time to see the soldier slammed to the ground by the enraged, hulking figure of Dan Dean. It was Corporal Reb Saunders and the gangly Texan came up as fast as he had gone down, his face flushed with anger and firelight.

"You had no right to do that, Dean," Reb shouted.

"I had ever right. I'm Carrie's father."

"There was nothin' to it, you old fool," Reb shot back, then he launched himself at Dan Dean.

The soldier's head caught the big man in the middle. There was an audible *oomph* and Dean was driven back against the wagon behind him. Reb Saunders had him around the waist still, but he was driven off by Dean's meaty fists.

No one seemed in a hurry to stop this fight. Ruff saw

Carrie Dean, her face buried in her hands, standing against a wagon. No one else showed much emotion. Men and women stood by, some with rifle in hand, just watching as Dean and the soldier went at it.

They were on the ground now, trading mostly wild, ineffective punches as they rolled toward the fire. Someone called out as they rolled over one last time and went into the fire ring, sending up sparks. Both men yowled and jumped up. Reb tried to take to his heels, but Dean tackled him and the corporal hit the ground again.

"Stop them!" Carrie Dean cried out.

Ruff considered it, but they didn't seem to be hurting each other much. Besides, he was feeling a little battered just then, and the other settlers, those cradling Winchesters and shotguns in their arms, didn't appear to want anyone interfering. They finally had one of the blue soldiers where they wanted him. They actually cheered now with each blow Dan Dean landed on the Texan, wanting to punish the army and every member of it.

The two men had fought their way across the clearing again with only Carrie Dean even wanting to stop it when Lieutenant Ed Sharpe and six armed soldiers finally showed up.

"What is this? Stop it. That's an order, Corporal Saunders," Sharpe shouted.

It wasn't easy for Reb to stop unless Dean did, and Dan Dean hadn't had his fill yet. His eyes were puffed, his nostrils leaking blood, his shirt ripped, knuckles skinned, but he wanted more.

"Corporal Saunders!"

Reb might not have even heard Sharpe that time. He had gotten his second wind and was busy pummeling the big man's face.

"Please!" Carrie Dean grabbed Sharpe's arm. "Stop them, Lieutenant!"

"I intend to," Sharpe said.

"Let 'em be," Caleb Updike said.

"What's the sense in it," Sharpe demanded, getting angry now.

"We'll see at least one of you bastards punished."

Maxwell was beside Updike and two other settlers, all armed. Ruff could see the anger and tension on their faces. It was reflected in the faces of the soldiers behind Sharpe. It was an ugly situation, and a unique one. The army patrol assigned to protect these civilians was in imminent danger of being assaulted by them.

Ruff Justice still hadn't taken a hand. Under the circumstances he didn't know what he could have done. No one spoke. The only sounds were the two men's bodies being struck by fists and feet, the puffing of their tortured lungs.

The two armies—for that is what they were—faced each other across the clearing. Sharpe took a step forward and said, "I'm ordering you people to break this up. Go back to your wagons."

"You're ordering no one," Caleb Updike said. "You don't see uniforms on my people, Lieutenant."

A rifle was cocked somewhere and then without an order all of the army rifles. Ruff bit at the inside of his lip. Ruth had appeared to grip his arm and stand gawking. Justice glanced at her, deciding which way they were going to move when the shooting started.

And then it did start.

7

The first shot seemed to come from the soldiers across the clearing, and Ruff flung himself backward. In the same instant he saw one of the settlers go down and realized that the rifle hadn't been fired from inside the camp at all.

A war whoop punctuated that realization. That and a scream of pain from beyond the wagons as the Cheyenne Indians hit the covered-wagon camp with guns spewing flame and death at the gathered whites.

The first few moments couldn't have been much worse. All of them, settlers and soldiers, had been gathered in a small area, standing around a fire, their attention on the fight. When the Indian rifles opened up, three or four people were hit before anyone even knew what had happened, where the danger had its source.

Later they said that one of the settlers in panic had shot a soldier and then been killed in turn by an Indian weapon, but no one could have been sure of that. It was chaos those first few minutes, and Ruff, diving beneath a wagon, taking Ruth with him, was no more certain than anyone else at first as to what had happened.

He had his Colt out as the Cheyenne leapt the wagon

tongue, his war lance held high, and Justice shot him through the chest from side to side. Blood spewed from the Indian's mouth and he fell from his horse to be trampled beneath its hooves.

"Marcia!" Ruth screamed, gripping Ruff's arm tightly as they lay side by side, watching the sporadic and confused fighting across the night camp. "We've got to get back to her."

"There's no assurance we'd make it."

"I can't leave her, Ruffin!"

Justice peered up, flinched reflexively as an arrow thudded into the wagon above them, and nodded. "All right. Let's make a try at it."

They rolled out the far side of the wagon, Ruff snatching Ruth to her feet, and made their run for the Dawkens' wagon. To the left the fighting had intensified. Ruff saw a woman lying dead on the ground, her dog nuzzling the body. Two soldiers fired at a target Ruff couldn't make out beyond the perimeter of the camp. Someone had wisely doused the fire, and smoke now drifted through the air like a ground fog creeping through the camp.

The Cheyenne on the painted war horse appeared directly in front of them. Ruth shouted—not screamed, but shouted—and Justice brought up the Colt in his hand, firing as the Cheyenne pulled the trigger on his army Springfield rifle.

He was just a kid, very young. He was never going to get any older. His bullet whipped past Ruff's ear and slammed into the side of a burning wagon. Justice's bullet hit home. It was a heart shot and it stopped the Indian's great life-giving muscle dead. He fell from the war horse as the animal swerved to avoid trampling Ruff and Ruth.

"It's afire!" Ruth shouted.

Ruff glanced that way and saw that her wagon was indeed on fire, the top going quickly, sending plumes of smoke, hot ash, and sections of burning canvas floating into the night sky.

"Marcia!" Ruth shouted above the crackling of the flames. The heat was intense. Ruff snatched an Indian blanket off the ground and went to the water barrel on the side of the burning wagon, soaking it, splashing water over his face and arms.

"You can't go in there," Ruth said, her fire-bright eyes wide, panicky.

"Got to," Ruff Justice said, and he nearly had to push her away.

He was to the burning tailgate in three strides, leaping up into the wagon as a segment of burning canvas fell around his head and shoulders like a fiery mantle. Ruff ducked low, holding the wet Indian blanket over his head with one hand. The blanket didn't do much good. It was hot as Hades; the smoke made it impossible to see. The floorboards burned underfoot.

Ruff, gasping, choking, leapt from the wagon as one of the axles went and it lurched sideways to lay against the ground, burning itself out.

"Marcia?" Ruth gripped his arm tightly when he returned to her side.

"Not there." Ruff shook his head.

"Thank God! How fortunate."

"Maybe," Ruff Justice said. He looked to the dark plains beyond the camp. Maybe she had been lucky—if the Cheyenne hadn't found her.

Ruth suddenly understood. "Oh, no!" Her hands went to her mouth.

"Take it easy—just because you fear something, that doesn't mean it's happened."

Ruff had his hands on her arms, and he could feel Ruth sag a little before pulling herself together to stand upright, looking into his eyes.

"Sorry, Ruffin."

"Don't be sorry, just don't let it get you."

"All right." She nodded meekly.

The shooting had died down across the camp and now it sputtered to a stop. The settlers and army people started to emerge from their hidey-holes to stand surveying the wreckage of the camp. Some of them had their mourning to do. Ruff counted six dead. Someone told him two of the pickets had gone down outside the camp. Eight altogether, then.

"Why didn't they finish us?" Sharpe wondered aloud.

"Small party. They'll be back. They didn't count on finding so many men standing around with guns in their hands. Fooled them, I'd guess."

"We didn't fool 'em much," Caleb Updike said. His red beard was singed, his face smudged. "We got dead and wounded."

"No, and we won't fool 'em again," Ruff said. "It's just that these people of Fox Fight's are young and mostly incautious. They proved they didn't have much experience."

"They won't need much if they come back," Sergeant Lew Walters grumbled. "Not if they've got a hundred braves."

"What do we do?" Sears Maxwell asked. The man looked beaten. He'd lost his daughter. His wife was mad. Now this—his wagon was one of the burned ones.

"It's not my decision," Ruff said. He glanced at Lieutenant Sharpe. "It's between you and the lieutenant here, Updike. But it's obvious you've got a short supply of options. Go ahead, right into their teeth, make a run for Lincoln—I doubt we'd make it, but it might offer a chance—head for Walker's Pass and try to fort up in the stage stop there, though we're too many."

"You're telling us we've got no options," one of the settlers shouted excitedly.

"No, I'm just telling you what they seem to be. They're not much, I admit."

"As a matter of fact, the only one we seem to have

now is to go ahead," Updike said. "The Cheyenne know where we are. We can't outrun them to the fort."

"I'd vote for Walker's Pass," another settler said. "Hold up there until the army cleans this Fox Fight out. If they can," he added, casting a disparaging glance at Sharpe.

"That might be months. It's already getting too late to seed a crop. If we don't get our corn in the ground this year, what'll we live on next year?"

Sharpe told them, "Take a vote. You decide among yourselves. There doesn't seem to be a good way to go. When you've made up your minds, tell me. I've got a burial detail to see to."

With that, Sharpe turned away. Ruff Justice went with him. "Where the hell is he?" Ruff wanted to know.

"Who?" Sharpe halted.

"Who? Tandy Monroe. When's the last time you saw him?"

"Why, I don't know. It's been some time, I guess. He must have gotten cut off—or been caught by the Cheyenne."

"I hope so. I don't know where he went or why, but it bothers me." Along with a few other things, like where Charity Blaine was. "I'll be back shortly," Ruff said.

"Oh—now where are *you* going?" Sharpe asked.

"To find a woman. I hope."

Justice shook his head. There was still smoke in the air. The night had a bitter taste to it. He could see Ruth standing near her still-burning wagon, wringing her hands, watching him expectantly. He turned sharply on his heel and went out into the darkness.

There wasn't much light, but gradually Ruff's eyes adjusted. He could see the sentries out now, double the usual number, and he found a dead man. A soldier whose name he'd never gotten. Ruff marked the location and told the next sentry he met.

Of the woman he found not a trace. He combed the area behind the wagon minutely, working his way out from the camp, at times getting to hands and knees to search, but there was just nothing.

That was what he had to tell Ruth when he got back to camp. She was standing pretty much where he had left her.

"What does it mean?" she asked warily.

"Mean?"

"She's not dead. She's not here."

"Maybe she's just wandered off and she'd gotten scared. She's hidden herself somewhere."

"Maybe the Cheyenne have her," Ruth said more logically.

Ruff nodded. "Maybe so. I'll look again when the sun comes up."

"That won't be long. Ruff, thanks for trying." Her hand touched his arm briefly and then fell away.

"There you are," Caleb Updike called. Ruth glanced at the red-bearded wagon master and walked away to poke through her belongings. There didn't look to be much there to salvage. "Where in hell've you been, Justice?"

"Out there. Didn't know anyone was looking for me."

"We've taken our vote. We're going to Walker's, to the stage stop."

"All right." Updike didn't look too happy about it. He was the one who wanted to get through to Bear Creek, wanted it badly.

"You'll have to lead the way. You've been down there once from here."

"Where's Tandy Monroe?"

"I wish I knew. Dead, I expect. Anyway, he's gone, you're our scout. And don't you worry about being paid right, Justice. I'll see that you're taken care of."

"With Leadville Bank money?" Ruff asked. He might

as well have kneed Updike in the groin. The man stiffened, his face suffusing with dark blood.

"You hear too much and you talk too much, Justice," Updike said threateningly.

"You're probably right," Ruff said. Then Updike turned and walked away into the darkness. He's got it with him, Justice thought. He's sure as hell got that bank money with him. No wonder he's so damned nervous.

What was his plan? The obvious one would be to repeat the Leadville experiment. Open a bank in Bear Creek, which was also a mining town. He had the cash to make it look good. It hadn't been real smart, Ruff decided, to let Updike become aware that Ruff knew his background.

There wasn't much time for playing games, however; he had been hoping to shake someone up, anyone who might know something about the murder of Katie Maxwell. Many things were possible—say Katie had seen Updike's stash of stolen money. Would he kill her over that? Maybe. It was all becoming academic anyway. Time was running out for Billy Sondberg. The kid wouldn't see many more sunrises.

Dawn broke through gathering clouds that Ruff eyed warily. All they needed was a good rain. The oxen were hitched hurriedly. Ruff made one last search of the area around the camp.

He found it on his last round as the sky went orange and then briefly flaming crimson. He swung down from the buckskin horse breathing a deep curse.

It was only one footprint, but it was very distinct in a bare patch of soil. It was small, sharp, a new boot. A woman's boot. And around it were dozens of tracks made by a pair of Indian moccasins.

"Got her," Ruff muttered. He stood, dusting his hands together, looking eastward. "God damn it all to hell."

And what was he supposed to do, let Fox Fight's people have her?

Ruff heeled his buckskin toward the soldiers, who were just beginning to mount up. Sharpe was there facing his men.

"What's up, Justice?"

"Cheyenne got a woman."

"What? Which woman?"

"The Dawkens girl. The hiding one. Marcia."

"Damn, and nothing we can do about it," the lieutenant said bitterly.

"Sure there is," Justice told him. "I'm going after her."

"Can't be done. If they haven't already cut her to pieces, they've got plans to. One man isn't going to take her away from Fox Fight's warriors."

"No. I don't think so."

"Then why. . . ?"

"Because I don't really think I can live with myself if I simply ignore the situation, Sharpe."

The army officer looked at the tall man sitting the buckskin horse. The wind drifted his long hair across his face. His eyes were cold and determined.

Sharpe shrugged. "What's the best way to get to the stage station at Walker's Pass?"

"You can't much miss it if you head for that small peak. But the wagons will have to cross the river this side of that stand of oaks you'll find beyond the rise. There's no ford farther down and the creek's running pretty good."

"All right. You're really going?"

"I'm really going."

Sharpe rested his hand on the neck of Ruff's buckskin. "Good luck, then . . . just good luck." And Sharpe turned away, bellowing a command at his men.

Ruff swung back to camp, finding Ruth near the wagon of another family that had consented to let her ride along. She hopped down and came to him, holding her skirts down as the wind toyed with them.

She saw it on his face. "Not dead!"

"No. Maybe worse. It looks like the Cheyenne have her," Justice told her.

"Oh, no! I knew it all along. I knew that was what happened, Ruff."

"All right. Take it easy now. I'm going to go get her and bring her back."

"You're going to what? The hell you are, Justice—I won't allow it."

"That's generous of you, but—"

"Generous, hell. You can't bring her back, and only a madman would try it."

"I've always been considered a little mad." He shrugged. He tried a smile on her, but it didn't work.

"No! I won't have it. If the Cheyenne have her, she's lost. Why should I lose you too?"

"Because it needs to be done, that's all," he replied.

She looked into his eyes deeply and then just shook her head, turning away. When she glanced back, she could only see Ruff's back as he rode his big buckskin from the camp.

"You're crazy, tall man," she whispered. "Crazy and very nice. And I don't think I'm ever going to see you again."

8

The wind was rising, ruffling the long grass before the hooves of Ruff's horse. Somber sentinel clouds stood high against the northern skies. From time to time distant thunder rumbled.

Five miles behind Justice was the wagon train, rolling to the doubtful security of the Walker's Pass stage stop. Ahead, the sheltering mountains cut stark silhouettes against the sky. Somewhere up there was Fox Fight, and a woman who wasn't much to look at, who had an edge to her voice and seemed to be filled with cotton batting instead of blood and flesh, but who didn't deserve to die at the hands of the Cheyenne.

Ruff rode with the Spencer unsheathed across his saddle. His eyes strained against the distances where the hills began to bunch together and press upward, stretching toward the high barren slopes above.

Somewhere up there the Indians would be watching.

They wouldn't expect anyone to be following, not a lone man at least, but they would be wary all the same. If the army could ever pinpoint Fox Fight's position, they would come after him with all they had. Fox Fight was no fool, he would know that. He wasn't quite ready to tackle the strength of the cavalry—not yet. He was playing a waiting game, pecking away at the settlers, the outposts, the cavalry patrols. It showed that Fox Fight was not completely crazy as some people were saying. He knew—he was a good general.

The cloud shadows began to darken the land as Ruff rode into the foothills. He could breathe a little easier, despite knowing that he was nearer yet to the Cheyenne stronghold. He had left the flat ground behind, the long plains where a moving man stands out starkly for mile upon mile. Among the folds and rises of the broken hills he could move with at least a slight feeling of confidence. From time to time he thought of Billy Sondberg, and mentally he apologized.

"They're going to shoot you, it looks like, kid. I can't help it. It's you or the woman. It's a damn shame, but that's the way it has to be."

It was more of a shame because Ruff at least knew now, or thought he did, why Billy Sondberg wouldn't speak up in his own defense.

It began to rain. At first, there were just a few scattered drops but then, as the drifting storm darkened the hill slopes, the skies opened up good. Ruff rode for a time and then was forced to swing down from the horse's back. The trail he had been following was an easy one—many horses ridden in a bunch. The rain would change that. With the tracks gone, Ruff would have little chance of ever finding the Cheyenne camp.

Not that they wouldn't be able to find him.

The skies got darker yet and the rain was cold and heavy. Lightning scored the mountain flanks above him and thunder echoed across the hills. Ruff was into pine forest now and the force of the wind and rain was blunted, but it was still uncomfortable moving through the trees.

He hadn't seen the Cheyenne's tracks for a good while now, despite twice circling back down the hillside to try cutting for sign. The pine needles underfoot didn't help things any, nor did the rain. The darkness that was now settling in earnest made it impossible. If there was a sun behind those dark thunderclouds, you couldn't prove it by looking. There was nothing but the whining wind, the constant army of pines emerging from the clouds and rain like giants with arms extended.

"No chance, horse. We've got to hole up."

It was that or wander farther from the track. He had no idea where he was going and the weather wasn't going to break until morning. Ruff took a slow breath. He would have stopped long ago, but there was a woman up here, one who had to be frightened, near panic, and there just wasn't anyone else to help her.

Ruff peered through the beads of rain that ran from his hat brim. He thought he saw, and then was sure he did see a stone face ahead of him through the pines and, rising vertically, a cleft in the wall. Wide enough to shelter him and the horse?

There was only one way to find out. He started toward it as thunder clapped again, near at hand. He swung down on reaching the stone face and led the buckskin toward it. The cleft was plenty wide, damp and cool, but not so damp and cool as the weather outside. It would do for the night's shelter. It would have to.

Ruff unsaddled and slipped the bit from the buckskin's mouth.

It was a miserable night. Justice had no fire, although in the cleft, with the storm wrapping its arms around the mountain, with the rain driving down, it was unlikely that anyone would have seen a fire unless he was standing right in front of it. Still, the scent of fire carries a long way, even in the rain, and Justice didn't feel like risking it. If he had to be cold to keep his hair for another night, then that was the way it would be.

He cleared aside some of the rubble—dead branches,

pack rats' nests, stones—and made a crude bed with his roll. He tied the buckskin to his wrist with a rawhide string. He didn't intend to lose that horse, not up here.

Then, after a few mouthfuls of jerky and dry biscuits washed down with canteen water, he fell to a fitful sleep and dreamed of satin sheets, silky women, and standing rib roasts.

There was no dawn, just a gradual graying of the world outside the cleft. Ruff Justice rose stiffly. The horse eyed him mournfully, accusingly

"I'm not any happier about it than you are," Justice said. The horse twitched its ears and got back to its accusing staring.

There was no choice about it—he would have to take it easy on the horse now and find some decent graze. He might travel all right on an empty belly, but the horse shouldn't have to. They went out into the gray drizzle of the morning.

Thunder rattled in the trees and the rain fell harder yet. Ruff was moving up a long cedar-covered slope, heading for a small pocket valley above him, a valley where the horse could find some grass and which offered Ruff a view of all the ground below him—or would have, if the clouds had ever parted. Below, white water frothed through a gray stone gorge. Nothing else seemed to live in the mountains then—there was only Ruff Justice and the elements.

That, of course, was an illusion.

The bullet whistled past in front of Justice's face and slammed into the cedar tree behind him, tearing out a fist-sized chunk of wood. Ruff dived from the saddle, hitting the ground hard, rolling into the trees as another shot and then another searched for him among the timber.

The buckskin was gone again. Damn that horse! Ruff lay in the rain, watching the slopes. Gray cold fog crept along the flanks of the mountains. The creek below hissed in its course, covering any other small sounds that might have carried to him.

Ruff had the big Spencer in his hands, his finger on the cool, curved steel trigger. At least one of the renegades would pay a price when they came looking for him. That big buffalo gun could give a man a hell of a bellyache.

But why didn't they come?

Ruff could see nothing of the Cheyennes. He would have expected to see them filtering through the woods, coming nearer and nearer, drawing his fire until they were near enough to make a certain thing of him.

Not Indians.

He was suddenly sure. Why, he didn't know exactly, but he was sure. That meant there was someone else on this mountain, another madman, for to be here was to invite death at the hands of Fox Fight's renegades.

The rifle spoke again, the bullet digging up a long furrow of earth. Justice sprang to one side. The next one tagged him. It tagged him low on the leg, a near miss, a burn across the calf, but it hurt like hell. It was like getting clubbed on the leg by a strong man. And it was bleeding pretty badly.

Justice hauled himself into a sitting position against the big pine at his back and he had a look at the leg. His hands were trembling as he rolled up his pants. Even a near miss like this one carries a tremendous shocking power. The body is stunned by the impact of lead against tissue and bone. Ruff wanted to shrug it off, just ignore it, but damn it all, it hurt. He sat there watching his leg bleed for a moment, watching the crimson of his blood mingle with the rain before he realized what he was doing—nothing.

Angrily he removed his scarf and knotted it around the wound. It wasn't much of a bandage but it would stanch the flow of blood a little. It would have to do, unless Justice was going to run across a pretty little nurse out here, and it didn't seem likely.

But someone was there.

Someone who wanted to kill Ruff, who wasn't himself an Indian but had no fear of being found by them. That made no immediate sense. The rifle fire sounded again, three shots. These were searching shots, intended to keep Ruff down and try for a lucky hit.

Justice had to move and he knew it. If he didn't, one of those bullets would find him again. He got to his belly and crawled slowly away from the tree, downslope toward the quick-running river as the rain drove down.

His leg was on fire, his head still a little giddy. He was cold and that stinking buckskin horse had taken off again on him.

He was also mad. He didn't enjoy being shot much. He had a .56-caliber Spencer repeating rifle, which he carried hopefully, wanting a good and proper use for the big gun.

He was nearly to the river now. No placidly running thing this wild mountain creek. It roared and thrummed down its channel, throwing up spumes of white water, licking at the gray stone around it. Ruff was on a stony ledge above the river peering down at it. Rain fell in a wash, making nearly as much noise as the river.

There was no way across at that point, and Ruff's mouth tightened. A mistake, and perhaps a costly one, but downslope seemed the best way for a man with a wounded leg who was going to have to take most of it on his belly.

Thunder volleyed across the storm-grayed day like a vast, menacing drumroll. Tandy Monroe burst from the trees above Ruff Justice, threw his rifle to his shoulder, and fired wildly three times.

"Damn you, Justice! I told you you'd die!"

The bullets from Monroe's Winchester whined off the stone around Justice, kicking up rock splinters.

Ruff moved instinctively. It was the right move, but it wasn't anything thought out. There wasn't time to roll over, sit up, bring the big Spencer to bear. He simply rolled the other way and dropped to the thundering river as Tandy Monroe's cries of frustration filled the air.

Justice somehow kept hold of his rifle, but it wasn't doing him much good. The river bulged against him and ripped at his limbs, slamming him past a shelf of rock and on downstream, ranting and fuming as it did so, as if its inability to spit out this foreign object had enraged the river god.

Justice was tumbled over and over. He gasped for breath, gulping it into his lungs at those rare moments when his head was above water. The trees fled by like a picket fence along the creek. The water was freezing, freezing. He no longer felt the pain in his leg.

And Tandy Monroe was far behind.

But that wouldn't do. Tandy couldn't be left there. Not now. He couldn't be left anywhere . . . alive. Ruff made that a solemn vow right then.

He was floating in a slower current, his head above water. Then his boot touched and he started struggling, half-swimming, half-walking toward the shore. He dragged himself up onto the bank and into the pines and stood shivering in the cold rain, soaked from head to foot.

Ruff stood looking, watching upriver through the mist and falling rain, seeing no sign of Tandy Monroe or any other pursuit. He couldn't make sense of this, and right now he was too cold to even think properly. All he knew was that Tandy didn't belong in these mountains alone, now.

Ruff's teeth chattered; his arms and legs were numb, hard with the cold. He went deeper into the forest, trying to stay alert, to keep his mind off the cold and wet. His buckskins weighed a hundred pounds. They dripped buckets of water. The lightning struck close at hand and Ruff sagged to the floor of the forest to sit there, shaking his head.

It was up, one way or the other. Going on like this, he was going to freeze to death.

If he was going to die, he might as well die warm. He still had that packet of oilskin-wrapped matches. He was going to have a fire and damn the Cheyenne.

Retreating farther up the hill slope, he found a sort of hollow, no more than a third of an acre across where time had scooped out a shelter. Timber rose on three sides. The fire would be virtually invisible—assuming he ever got one started.

And he had to. He just had to. He was going to have to start one and keep it going. Well, and the renegades could just come along and roast him over it.

He pulled the loose bark off of a dying spruce and shredded the dry inner bark. That was his tinder. Ruff crouched over it in the rain, up against a shelf of rock that disguised the fire even more and broke the wind.

He unwrapped his waterproof box of matches and struck one. It caught, fizzled, and went out. Justice had three left and his mouth tightened. He managed to get the tinder going with the next match, bent low over his fire, puffing on it gently. It caught, sending up a thin tendril of smoke and a following tongue of bright flame.

Ruff poked at the fire with a few dry twigs pried from a crack in the rock, dug up from below the lowest layer of ancient pine needles where they had begun to decompose. They were dry, nearly powdery, burning with a bright-yellow flame.

Ruff stripped off his boots and buckskins and hung them on a dead branch thrust into the crack in the stone wall. They steamed and hissed over the fire. He could still feel the rain, its force blunted by the trees overhead. Ruff crouched next to the fire, naked, long-haired, warming slowly, as savage and primitive as any man who had ever crouched over a fire in these lonesome mountains—except for the .56 Spencer in his hand.

The Colt was a lost cause after being soaked in the river, but there was a chance the powder in the .56 cartridges was dry. With the skinning knife from his boot, Ruff pried the big bullet from a cartridge and sprinkled a little powder out into his palm.

Dry. Smiling tightly, he tossed the powder into the fire and watched it whoosh and smoke, then tossed the cartridge away.

There's enough for Tandy anyway, Ruff thought.

All the ammunition he had was what was in the Spencer—six shots now. That would do for Tandy Monroe if he ever showed up, but it wasn't going to hold off Fox Fight's men.

Ruff crouched there thinking dark thoughts, staring down the slope. He thought of Tandy and of Fox Fight, bitter and blood-crazed, of Ruth Dawkens and the quick warm clasp of her thighs, of Caleb Updike and his embezzled bank funds, of Sears Maxwell and his grief-maddened wife, of a kid he hardly knew sitting helplessly in a small dark stone cell at Fort Lincoln.

And of Marcia Dawkens.

Twisted, bitter, old before her time. Now the Indians had her. If Ruff found her at all, he would likely find her dead; if alive, she would likely be a physical and emotional wreck.

Those ifs were a long way off just then to the man who sat over the tiny fire, eyes brooding, deep, mouth tight with anger and hatred.

The buckskins weren't dry when Ruff started on; they would never be dry until the rain stopped, but Ruff had gained a temporary respite from the bitter cold.

He trudged onward, upslope, trying to figure out why he didn't just give it up and get the hell out of there. Who was he helping with this business? Maybe it was pride that drove him on. He often thought of that. He was counted a brave man, but maybe a man with that reputation has to keep on being brave, to continue to build his own reputation in his mind's eye. Maybe there's no end to it until the bravery becomes sheer recklessness and you go out still carrying that reputation.

He was a brave man.

"That profits you," Ruff muttered aloud. He clamped his jaw shut on the brief bitter monologue, closed the doors in his mind that allowed such misgivings to flit through.

He came up over the jagged ridge where time had eroded the soil beneath the pines and revealed the saw-toothed, uptilted rock beneath it.

He could see hundreds of miles of virgin forest, see the great bulking mountains. And nearly at his feet he cold see the village of the Cheyenne renegades.

9

The rain had lifted, the clouds opening like dramatic curtains. Now they closed around Ruff Justice and the mountaintop again, folding him into their chill. His blood was touched by the chill, running cold through his veins.

Fox Fight.

Now, if he only had a troop of cavalry or two . . . He had six rounds in his Spencer carbine and a bowie knife. He had a wounded leg, no horse to escape on, no idea of how this thing could be done.

All he had was the need to do it.

"Likely the woman's dead," he told himself. He nodded. Very likely. On his way down the wooded slope toward Fox Fight's camp, he decided that it was almost a certainty.

The rain fell. Ruff was cold again, as cold as he had been in the river. The clouds moved darkly across the land, rumbling and gusting, fitfully stretching damp, powerful muscles.

The Cheyenne were keeping close to their camp. Ruff lay in the timber atop a small, nearly smooth granite ledge, watching the activity in the village, what little there was of it.

There were no women in this camp, no children, dogs, or old people. Their lodges were mostly lean-tos, with here and there a tepee. The war ponies were up a narrow valley opposite, watched by two Cheyenne. At least Ruff saw two of them. They were two too many for him.

In the camp itself he saw no unusual goings-on as he would have expected if half a hundred of the renegades had decided to rape Marcia Dawkens. But there weren't half a hundred here. That Delaware scout must have had double vision. The colonel would be happy to hear the news—if he ever got it.

Ruff heard the moccasins on the ground behind him. How he did above the rain and wind was remarkable, but he had an instinct for survival, and the Indian was not trying to be cautious.

He was simply another of the world's bored, weary soldiers making a slow cold round of the camp perimeter, expecting to meet no one, thinking only of food and fire and of a woman back home.

He should have been thinking a little more of his work.

Ruff remained crouched, his hair in his eyes, but his bowie had been slipped from its beaded sheath to fill his hand with its cool comfort. The Cheyenne looked skyward and then toward the camp.

He never saw Justice spring up and strike for the throat, never saw the dull flash of the bowie's blade as it severed the arteries there. The Cheyenne slumped to the ground, strangling in his own blood.

Justice hunched over the body, looking right and then left. There was nothing moving but the clouds across the mountain slope. He hurriedly pulled the Cheyenne into the deeper woods, covered the body with brush as best he could, then lifted the renegade's blanket from the ground.

Maybe in this weather . . . Ruff didn't think about it

much longer; he just wrapped the blanket around his shoulders and started along the ridge, his rifle in his hands. From a distance he might fool someone. For a time.

It was starting to get dark. A few fires were lighted in the Cheyenne camp. How long before someone came to relieve the Indian Ruff had killed?

Justice waited another anxious hour and then started down through the trees toward the camp itself. The biggest tent would almost certainly be Fox Fight's. Maybe not, but it was a good bet.

In the darkness of the night Ruff nearly walked into a renegade Indian. The man didn't even speak, brushing hurriedly past Ruff, who stood for a moment, heart pounding.

Turning again toward the camp, Ruff put the blanket over his head, drawing it partially across his face to cover it. There were very few Cheyenne warriors with mustaches. Keeping to the shadows, he moved around the perimeter of the camp, expecting a cry of alarm at any moment—someone would have to discover that body sooner or later.

The rain came in again, in a powerful, drenching downpour that Ruff would have cursed heartily early in the day, but that now cheered him. It was difficult to see five feet in front of you.

The tepee loomed suddenly just that far in front of Ruff's eyes.

There were magic signs on the tent and, inside, a fire was burning, dimly, smokily illuminating the buffalo hide of the tepee, throwing occasional sparks into the sky through the tent flap.

Ruff looked around cautiously. His heart had lifted itself into his throat and wedged there. He could see no one. He could hear voices, however. Faint, muffled.

They spoke in English.

The storm twisted and bent the words, but a few

syllables came through, a word here and there. One of the voices was a man's—and he was an Indian.

The other voice Ruff Justice recognized instantly. Harsh, strident, it belonged to Marcia Dawkens.

". . . to eat. To warm the belly on a night such as—"

"No, thank you. If you think—"

"Death, you understand . . . for a man like me."

"I really have no interest in—"

Ruff frowned. He stood in the rain, blanket over his head, listening. The little conversation continued, but there were only the two voices, perplexing Ruff. Marcia Dawkens was giving as good as she got. Fox Fight seemed puzzled by it, or perhaps astonished was a better word.

"I have . . . the white soldiers . . . and cut their tongues out of their lying throats. With my army . . ."

He continued beating his chest for a while. Marcia Dawkens—indomitable, apparently—had no interest at all in this masculine business of boasting.

". . . sleep here!" Ruff heard her rising voice shout. "You will have to return me . . ."

He would have to do that if Justice had anything to say about it, but it didn't seem that he did. There was no way he was going to escape this camp, no way he could get horses . . . Well, maybe just one way.

Ruff Justice walked to the tepee flap, stepped into the smoky firelit interior, and wheeled back the hammer on the big Spencer, letting the muzzle drift toward Fox Fight's belly.

"Who are you?" The Indian started to get up and Ruff jabbed him hard with the rifle barrel. He sat down again, hard, holding his belly.

"Where have you been, Mister Justice?" Marcia Dawkens demanded.

"I got lost."

"This hasn't been pleasant. May we go?" she asked, and Ruff could only stand looking at her.

"We're going to try. First of all, kick that rifle there aside." Ruff nodded at Fox Fight's new Winchester, which had been decorated with brass nails. "That's right. Now move in behind him and lift that knife from his waistband."

"You will die, white," Fox Fight spat.

"Sure. So will we all. You want your end to come now?"

Fox Fight continued to sit and stare at the muzzle of that .56 rifle. No, he wasn't ready to die yet.

"Well, what are we waiting for," Marcia snapped. She had a few smudges of dirt on her face and her hair was disarranged, but she didn't appear to have been roughed up much, if at all. Fox Fight on the other hand had scratches on his face, which could only have been made by fingernails.

"We need horses, Fox Fight," Ruff said with careful deliberateness. "We're going to circle around behind the camp and you're going to find three horses for us. Then we're riding east. All of this has to be done right, understand?"

"If not?" the Cheyenne asked, holding his head high.

"You die." Ruff shrugged. He found a length of rawhide bow wrapping in the corner of the tepee and he gave Marcia his rifle to hold on Fox Fight.

Ruff tied the rawhide around his own wrist, then around the renegade's wrist. Fox Fight watched him haughtily. Outside, it continued to rain and the wind blew unabated. The camp seemed quiet, but these were men at war and they would not all be sleeping soundly.

"What now?" Marcia asked, handing Ruff back his gun.

"Now we go."

"Can't we wait until it stops raining."

Justice just stared. He stared into the twisted face of Marcia Dawkens, and wondered what forces of nature had formed such a thing. Was she simply mad? Ruff wasn't discounting that yet.

"No. We have to go now," he said. Ruff looked at Fox Fight, nearly feeling sorry for the man. "Move it, Fox Fight."

"What?"

"It's too late for the 'no-speak' routine, Fox Fight. You speak plenty. A fine reservation education. You listen to me and do what I say."

"Never back to reservation!"

"Out of here, damn you, then I don't care if they hang you or you fight until they find you riddled with bullets."

"If you knew the reservation . . ."

"I know 'em too well, but I'm not here to talk about that situation. Is what you're doing supposed to be helping the people on the reservations?"

Fox Fight was silent. His only answer would have been raw anger. Well, Justice could understand that. He had once spent time on a reservation, trying to manage it. That was down in Apache country, but the problems were the same. He had sympathy for the people who lived on those ill-conceived places, but he wasn't going to sit and commune with Fox Fight about the inadequacies of the reservations just now.

"Move it," was what Ruff said, and Fox Fight, snatching up a blanket, moved out into the cold and rain.

They walked behind the tepee and then into the trees quickly, Ruff not wanting to risk crossing the camp directly. They moved through the storm quietly, hurriedly. Ruff could feel the occasional tug on his wrist as Fox Fight got a little too far away, and he would jerk him back, needing to keep him close.

Without Fox Fight they were dead.

"I don't see why we have to—" Marcia Dawkens began. Ruff cut her off curtly.

"Shut up."

"Well, if I'd known—"

"Shut up or I'll hit you over the head and carry you out of here," Ruff warned her, and she knew he wasn't kidding. She didn't like it, but she shut up.

The mouth of the wooded canyon suddenly yawned at them from out of the darkness. Fox Fight was just ahead of Ruff as they approached the two wet sentries there, and Ruff whispered his warning.

"The wrong word's the last."

"You will die."

"Yes. I will die *too*."

Fox Fight said nothing. Ruff held his blanket across his face again. The two sentries stared at the three of them, but the seeing wasn't too good on this night. They saw Fox Fight, an unidentified warrior, and the woman captive, and thought nothing more about it.

"My paint pony and two others," Fox Fight was saying. Ruff was listening intently. He spoke the Cheyenne tongue, but was well aware that any native speaker can find ways of confusing a non-native's ear. Simply speaking rapidly was one way. Fox Fight didn't attempt any tricks. He recalled the thumb-sized bore of that buffalo rifle Ruff carried.

There was a brief discussion, however. "Snake," the sentries kept repeating. "Snake would not like it."

Justice didn't get it. It was a man's name, but it meant nothing to him. It seemed that this Snake was another high-ranking renegade, but Justice hadn't heard any talk of the man before this moment.

Fox Fight was either a good actor or he was genuinely infuriated by references to Snake. "Get the ponies and be still," he told the warriors, and there was anger in his voice.

One of the sentries walked up the canyon and returned with three horses while the other stood moodily by, his back to them and to the rain, which seemed to have settled in for the night now.

Fox Fight took the lead line to all three ponies and they walked slowly away, Ruff expecting, dreading, a sudden warning shout, a flurry of bullets, the final impact of lead against flesh. After all, what did Fox Fight have to lose? He must have expected Ruff to kill him once they got free of the camp—or at best to be returned to the fort, where he would be hanged as all renegades were.

There was no shot, just the crackling of distant lightning. Once into the trees, they mounted, Ruff still tied wrist-to-wrist with Fox Fight, and they clapped heel to the ponies, riding upslope into the shelter of the storm, the forest, the night.

It rained the night through, which was good in that it would cover their tracks—not that Ruff was discounting the ability of the Cheyenne to find him. They were just too good at this business, practicing since childhood at tracking game that their tribe depended on. But it would be slow going. As long as they could stay reasonably well ahead, the Cheyenne wouldn't catch up.

"There could be others out here," Marcia said as she jerked along on the back of the roan horse she was riding.

"There could be."

"Once the sun is up, they'll be able to see us for a long way."

She was right again, and Ruff commented on her acumen. Marcia sniffed a little and rode in silence for a while.

"How was my sister?" she asked later as they walked the horses through the damp, deep pines.

"Fine." Was she now? Ruff didn't know. That wagon train had already been hit once by Fox Fight's men. Had they returned? He would have asked the Indian leader, but he had no reason to expect the truth out of Fox Fight.

"We'll not be able to outrun them," Marcia said.

"We will. Keep riding."

"You don't understand. My horse has gone lame."

Ruff swung down, cursing and growling. Fox Fight, still tethered to Ruff, sat his horse in the darkness, silent and unmoving.

It was the right front. A ligament was badly bowed. The roan wasn't going to put much weight on it for a time. Ruff sat back on his heels and looked skyward, cursing silently but profusely.

"It was when we crossed the little creek. The rocks this side of the . . ." Marcia wanted to talk about it. The woman, who was normally shrill and voluble, had become a confidante and pal. There was some perverse side of Marcia Dawkens that was enjoying this night of excitement. But then, Ruff was realizing, she was very likely mad.

"Get up with me, then," Ruff told her, and she did, with alacrity. She wrapped her arms around Ruff's waist and leaned her head against him as he started his horse forward once more.

The night was long and cold, but dawn came far too soon. Gray skies in the east promised first light, and with first light the Cheyenne would be on their trail.

They were stuck, good and stuck.

"I thought you had a plan," Marcia said.

"It sort of petered out at this point," Justice said peevishly.

Beyond the next rise were the gradually flattening foothills that degenerated into the plains. The plains obviously couldn't be crossed in daylight, rain or no. Not with the three of them on two weary mounts.

Ruff's eyes had been searching the hills and now he lifted a finger hopefully. "What's that?" he asked.

"Where?" Now it was Marcia who was peevish. Her unequal eyes followed Ruff's line of sight to a plateau where pine grew thickly to a prominent headland.

"To the left of that declivity, where the white limestone breaks off."

"I'm sure I don't know. I don't what it has to do with us," Marcia commented with a sniff. But Ruff was ignoring her now.

"Do your people know that place, Fox Fight?" Ruff asked, getting no answer. It was very possible they didn't. The Cheyenne weren't native to these hills. Maybe they had never seen the cave, if that was what it was.

"You can't mean you are thinking of taking shelter up there?" Marcia asked.

"Yes. Why not?"

"We should be running for the wagon train."

"I'd like to, but that's what they expect and we'd never make it. We're going to have to hide out for a while, till dark."

And again Ruff Justice silently apologized to Billy Sondberg. As critical as this time was to Ruff, it was more critical to Sondberg, sitting in the shade of the gallows.

Ruff lifted his eyes to the headland and started his weary pony forward once more. Fox Fight followed, looking very unconcerned—but then, why would he worry? Justice wasn't exactly a huge threat to his tribe or to himself. He only said it once, as Ruff recalled, but he was absolutely right.

"This is no good. The only way out of these hills for you, Ruff Justice, is through death's door."

10

The mouth of the cave had vanished as they rode up a tricky, rocky switchback. The trail became a narrow, broken path up the face of the headland. From there it was possible to look out over the mountains for many miles, to see the white river racing toward the flats.

"It's straight down," Marcia complained.

Ruff glanced past the horse's shoulder and he was forced to agree. "Straight down."

"You don't know where you're taking us, do you?"

"No," he replied. "I don't."

He hoped he was leading them to that cave or at least to a vantage point from which they could see their back trail and be reasonably safe until dark.

"And how are we going to get down this in the dark?" Marcia demanded.

The woman asked some good questions.

Sunrise flushed the peaks to red-violet and brought the valleys into shadowed relief. The pines were deep blue-green beneath the closing skies.

Ruff looked upward still, guessing, hoping that they were moving toward the cave. The Cheyenne, he thought, would have no interest in, or use for, this trail. They were in the hills to hide, to have a place to strike from. Likely they weren't aware of the cave's existence—Ruff had just happened to glance up, to need at that time a shelter. Another half-mile on and the cave had vanished from sight.

"This trail—it's something from out of the bowels of time," Marcia said.

"Ancient, very ancient," Justice agreed. The stone was weathered and crumbling. Someone, once, had built this trail for reasons Justice could only guess at—some people who had come and gone before the Cheyenne and the Utes.

Fox Fight made his move.

They rounded a sharp left-hand turn in the trail, and he leaped from his horse. Justice went over with him, tethered as they were wrist-to-wrist, and when they hit the ground, they hit hard.

Ruff's horse reared up on the narrow trail, its hooves slashing dangerously close to the two men. Ruff woozily got to his feet. To his right was a drop-off of a thousand feet and then some.

Fox Fight had his rifle.

Savage triumph illuminated the renegade leader's dark features. Justice didn't even take a breath before he reacted. He dived at Fox Fight's feet, taking that for his only chance. The big rifle spoke once, spitting smoke and lead into the canyon below. The horses, crazed by the shot on that narrow trail, whickered wildly and bucked. Marcia was hanging on to the horse's neck for dear life.

Fox Fight had gone down so hard that, as Ruff cautiously rose, his bowie at Fox Fight's throat, the fight was already over. The Cheyenne was out cold. Blood ran freely from a gash across the side of his head where it had struck stone. Justice stood unsteadily, glanced back to see if Marcia was all right, and picked up his big rifle.

"They'll have heard that shot," the woman said.

"I'm afraid so."

"And they'll be coming." She looked back down the long canyon, her blond hair twisting around her face as the wind gusted. She came forward a step or two and looked down at the unconscious Cheyenne. "He's hurt badly, isn't he?"

"Not too bad."

"Can't we stop the bleeding?"

Ruff, who had been peering into the distances trying to see, fearing to see pursuit, looked back at the woman with curiosity. There was real concern on her face, sorrow perhaps.

"Don't you even care about him?" she asked.

Ruff had compassion for his fellow man, but it didn't quite extend to butchers like Fox Fight. "He'll be all right."

Marcia's eyes were accusing, uncomprehending. Justice picked Fox Fight up roughly and slung him over the back of the paint pony. Then with a nod, Justice started on, leading the paint while Marcia stared after him, her crooked face twisted by conflicting thoughts and emotions.

The cave was there, set back from the gray stone ledge where the trail ended. Ruff led the horses inside, startling a cloud of thumb-sized bats into dark, frantic motion. Marcia bit at her lip, fighting back the disgust. Justice wondered what primitive instinct caused that fear in so many people around bats.

"Is there room?" she asked.

"Plenty of room." His voice echoed back to him.

"It's damp. And we won't have a fire."

"No fire."

Justice unloaded Fox Fight and put him on the stone floor of the cave, near the mouth so that what light there was on this gray day shone in on him. He cut the rawhide tether loose from his own wrist and tied Fox

Fight's hands behind his back. The Cheyenne moaned a little as Ruff moved him.

"Is it necessary to tie him?" Marcia asked.

"Probably. I'm doing it," Justice answered. Then he rose and walked out onto the windswept ledge to peer over the edge and down onto the trail. From there it looked even steeper, narrower. No one on horseback was going to sneak up that trail. Looking up, Justice could see the heads of masses of pine trees as they swayed in the wind, bent out to peer into the canyon, and then straightened. A lone crow sailed against the cold sky.

"Is there a way out up there?" Marcia asked.

"That's what I intend to find out right now." He handed her his rifle.

"Watch Fox Fight."

"He's unconscious!"

"Maybe. Maybe he'll even stay that way, but if he doesn't, you may want the gun."

"No. I couldn't use it."

"All right." Justice shrugged. "You want to climb up with me?" He nodded toward the highlands.

"No. I'm too tired anyway. I'll stay and watch him."

"Watch him close. Don't untie him, woman. No matter what."

"You can trust me," she said stiffly.

"That's good. Don't have too much sympathy for that man—maybe in his own world he's a hero and not a killer, but he still doesn't mind murdering folks, especially white folks."

"He's never so much as threatened me," Marcia said stridently, "and that is more than I can say for some other men of whom I have made recent acquaintance!"

Ruff grinned. What else could he have done? "Don't untie him," he repeated.

She watched him, hands on hips, until he had crossed the ledge and started up the chute beside the cave. It was narrow, time-worn, crumbling. Could a horse scramble up it? Maybe. Justice himself was having a hard time. He looked up into the gray skies, at the rubble-strewn chute. He could barely make out the serrated tip of a lone pine tree and he worked his way toward it, rocks bounding downslope behind him as he went.

It took another fifteen minutes with much sliding back and barking of knees before he was up and onto the headland where the wild winds blew and all of the world seemed at his feet. He skirted the edge of the promontory, walking into the wind. The rain began again, sporadically, hurling handsful of drops against his face. He didn't want to leave Marcia down there alone too long, but he needed to know if there was a way out of this—or if he had simply devised his own death trap.

He stopped abruptly, a map in his mind, an old map coming into conformation with what he now saw. It was backward, somehow tilted, but Ruff knew the area he was looking down into now.

Walker's Pass.

Squinting into the wind and weather, he could make out what looked to be the dark canyon that ran up behind the stage stop itself—the stage stop where Lieutenant Sharpe had been headed with the wagon train. He stared until his eyes ached, trying to make out a horse, the white top of a wagon, anything that might tell him if they had reached Walker's Pass and comparative, if temporary, safety. But he could make out nothing. The huge grove of oaks around the stage stop appeared only as a dark pinpoint. A hundred wagons could be in that grove.

One thing he did know: they could beat the Cheyenne trackers to that stage stop. The Indians had miles to go, over the foothills and then across the plains. They could drop down out of there and even if the horses had to be abandoned, they could make it to Walker's Pass in twelve hours, maybe much less.

"It's going to have to be in the dark, though," Ruff said, looking to the skies, cursing the storm. With a moon they had a reasonable chance of getting down off the mountain on this side, With starlight it wasn't all that bad. With the dark of a mountain storm it was going to be tricky.

Still, it had to be after dark—the Cheyenne were too near.

Having made the decision, Ruff quit worrying about it. It wasn't going to do him any good. There was only one way to go, one time to go. He mapped the land mentally as well as he could and then started back toward the cave as the skies rumbled again and the rain began in earnest.

He found Marcia hunched over the wounded Fox Fight. He surprised them coming in and caught the astonishing look of tenderness on the woman's face as she dabbed at the scalp wound on the renegade leader's head.

She spun around angrily, aware from Fox Fight's expression that someone was there. Ruff Justice shrugged and, moving to the opposite side of the cave mouth, squatted down. From there he could see the head of the trail leading to the cave. Almost see it, for his eyes were blurred with the need for sleep. He could get along with very little of it, had always been that way, but it had been a long while since he had slept now, a long ride and walk, a lot of tension. His eyes drooped a little.

"Is there a way?" Marcia asked. He could hear her tearing off strips of her petticoat to use for bandages.

"There's a way."

"When?"

"After dark."

"Mister Justice, when we get back, what happens to Fox Fight?"

"I don't know. The government gets him."

"They'll kill him."

"Likely."

Marcia settled into an angry silence. Fox Fight looked vaguely amused.

"We've only got two horses," Marcia said as she carefully wound the bandage around the Indian's head.

"That's right."

"Well, there's the three of us. We could go faster if only we two—well, what good is he to us?"

Ruff had been shaking his head through her little speech. "We need him to stay alive. If the Cheyenne catch up, we have a hostage."

"That will do you no good," Fox Fight said.

"What are you talking about?"

"Me—as a hostage. If they come, and I am not so sure they will, there are those who would not mind seeing me die as well in a gun battle. It could always be blamed on you."

"Are you talking about this Snake?"

"Yes." The Cheyenne nodded. "Snake."

Marcia stood, asking, "What is this?"

"There seems to be a little power struggle among the renegades. Fox Fight has been holding on to leadership, but now there's a buck named Snake who wants to unseat him. Is that about it?"

"That is it. Snake says my magic is not so good."

"Do you mean they won't even follow?" Marcia asked.

"I do not know," Fox Fight said. "Maybe. Although Snake would only be pleased to see me given over to the army, to be hung."

Outside, the rain came down heavily, the skies going nearly black. Ruff sat near the cave entrance, feeling the cold wind tug at his body. Better and better, he thought. There was a chance Snake might not even try to get Fox Fight back. There was some small hope of surviving this night and the next day after all.

"What was Tandy Monroe doing up here?" Ruff asked.

"Tandy Monroe sells things," Fox Fight said with a smile.

"Yes? Like what?"

"Whatever it is that we wish," the renegade said.

"People?"

"Certainly."

"I don't get this," Marcia complained. Her crooked features were softened and flattered by the shadows. She looked very much like Ruth at certain angles. Her voice, however, was still harsh, grating. Fox Fight didn't seem to mind. He sat there gazing at her ... and tugging at the rawhide bonds holding his wrists together. Ruff would have to tighten them later.

"I think I understand," Ruff Justice told her. "A guide doesn't make all that much money. Tandy's getting old for it. It's hard work, hard country. He somehow hit on a plan where he could make plenty of money being a guide.

"I once saw Tandy lose a party of settlers in a way that was so incompetent it went beyond belief. Hard weather killed them, most of them, and then the Indians came down and looted the wagons. It wasn't incompetence. Tandy did it on purpose."

"Killed an entire wagon train full of people!"

"More than once. The weather isn't reliable enough. Tandy decided to bring the wagon trains directly to Fox Fight and he set that up with your friend here. The wagons would roll right up to wherever Fox Fight wanted them. The ambush the other night was set up by Tandy—that was why he was nowhere around when it happened. It was partly my fault. Tandy wanted to take an unusual but good-enough route and I didn't think it was worth quibbling over. I should have quibbled.

"Something went wrong with that raid, though. We got off lucky. Someone got impatient to count coup—Snake?"

Fox Fight nodded. "He wished to bring many scalps. He was supposed to wait. Why didn't you kill him that night!" Savagery flashed in Fox Fight's dark eyes and then faded out.

"I knew something was wrong when I saw Tandy in these hills. No white with anything like Monroe's experience was going to come wandering around up here with the Cheyenne like they are, and that meant only one thing: Tandy was working with the Indians."

"You're very good at figuring things out," Marcia Dawkens said.

"Yeah," Ruff agreed, "when it's too damn late to help anything."

It was full dark when they started out. Full dark and moonless. The stars bled thin blue light through the gaps in the clouds, but it wasn't much help. The chute hadn't seemed that bad in daylight, afoot. Looking at it now, with the horses to consider, it seemed almost mad.

"A long climb, Justice," Fox Fight said. There was some mockery in his voice, but some real interest too. Maybe all warriors are logicians to some extent. Fox Fight must have solved many problems of troop movement, materiel transportation in his brief career as a general.

"Do you feel up to climbing it?" Ruff asked.

"With my hands tied?"

"Afraid so."

Fox Fight laughed. "If I must."

Marcia didn't like the idea and said so pointedly. "It's barbaric. He can't possibly do it without the use of his hands, Justice."

"He'll try. I'm not cutting him loose."

Temporarily, in fact, Fox Fight was going to be tied even more. Using still more off the bottom of Marcia's petticoat, Justice tied the Indian's ankles tightly. The woman stood by watching with disgust.

"I'm not sure who the barbarian is," she snapped.

"Neither am I," Ruff was willing to admit. "I'm just trying to stay alive, lady, and to keep you alive. If we have to be a little barbaric, then that's the way it's got to be."

Ruff left her with her concerns for his soul and took the lead reins for the ponies. He walked to the chute and stared upward into the darkness, trying to reconstruct things in his mind. He patted the paint on the neck, took a slow breath, and started up.

The horses' hooves clattered on the stone. Small rocks bounded away, ringing off the walls of the chute. The paint went almost immediately to its knees. In the starlight Ruff could see the whites of its wide eyes, as he jerked it to its feet again. The other pony misstepped and dragged them all back down the slope in a shower of stone. Gritting his teeth, Ruff started up again, urging, pleading, coaxing the horses.

Somehow he made it up with both horses intact. He stood panting, leaning against a great pine, his body bathed in sweat, chilled by the gusting wind. The horses stood together, flanks heaving.

Ruff started back down.

He cut Fox Fight's ankles free and let the Indian stand while circulation returned. "I'd ditch those petticoats, were I you, Miss Dawkens."

"Why?" she demanded.

"The climbing's going to be hard. They'll encumber you."

"Very well," she said curtly. "Turn your backs please."

They did, Fox Fight actually smiling. They heard a brief rustling sound and then Marcia Dawkens announced, "I'm ready now, Justice."

They started up the stony chute, Marcia going first, Fox Fight next, with his hands tied in front of him.

110

Ruff trailed, his rifle slung crudely across his shoulder with a rawhide strap. The rocks that the two above him kicked free bounced past Ruff's head. From time to time he had to move quickly to avoid a good-sized one. Marcia Dawkens slipped and fell repeatedly. Climbing in the darkness wasn't easy, but she stuck with it, drawing Ruff's admiration.

Marcia was already over the top of the chute and Fox Fight nearly there when he tried it again.

The Cheyenne turned suddenly and in his hands was a head-sized boulder. Ruff saw the glint in Fox Fight's eyes, saw the grimace on the Indian's face. He threw himself to one side as the rock, hurled at his head, whistled past. Fox Fight tried to get another rock as the first clattered harmlessly off down the chute, but before he could pick one up, Justice was all over him.

Ruff grabbed the Cheyenne's ankle, took a kick to the temple, and swung out with a fisted hand, catching the Indian on the jaw. Fox Fight struck back, throwing his knee up to try to keep Ruff off him, clubbing at Justice with both of his hands. Both men slid back down the chute as Justice hooked twice to the side of the Indian's head. The second blow put him out.

They had halted their skid thirty feet down the slope. Ruff lay still, catching his breath. His knee ached and his wounded leg had torn open again. He looked up and saw the pale face of Marcia Dawkens peering curiously down at them.

With a sigh and a curse, Ruff started up, dragging Fox Fight behind him up that endless chute.

"What did you do to him?" Marcia asked as Ruff finally rolled up and over onto the flats. He pulled Fox Fight up behind to lie on the grass moaning, holding his belly and head, kicking a foot in pain and frustration.

Justice had rolled him over and retied the hands behind Fox Fight's back. Marcia was on her knees cooing over the Indian, her twisted face softened by concern. Very touching.

"I wish my sister knew just how vicious you are," Marcia Dawkens said.

Ruff just nodded. Cold sweat stung his eyes. His hands, his elbows, his knees, were torn by the rocks. His head rang from Fox Fight's kick. His leg, where Tandy Monroe had shot him, hurt like hell. It was bleeding again. He felt particularly vicious as he tied the last knot and sagged to the earth.

They stayed on the ground, the three of them getting their breath back, letting the spinning dots in their heads be subdued by sufficient oxygen.

When Ruff's own heartbeat had slowed to a reasonable pace and Marcia looked strong enough, he stood. "Ready?" he asked. "Can we go on?"

"Yes." Marcia took his arm and rose. Her anger had faded a little. They both helped Fox Fight to his feet. They had already started for the horses when they heard it.

It was an eerie, distant sound, a sound Justice had heard on and off for the past few nights. The sound of a coyote calling to the limitless distances, to the vast and incomprehensible spirits of endless night.

But, as before, it was no coyote.

"What is it?" Marcia asked as the two men looked toward the west expectantly.

Fox Fight answered. "Snake. He comes."

11

❖

The land was broken and dark. The rain fell hard as Ruff Justice led the small party down through the pines toward what he hoped would be the security of the Walker's Pass stage stop, still miles distant over rough country Justice didn't know.

Behind them came the Cheyenne. What Snake would do with Fox Fight out here in the darkness was anyone's guess. What he would do with Justice and the woman was certain.

"Snake wanted to kill me, you know," Marcia told Justice.

"Did he?"

"Fox Fight stopped him. Doesn't that prove something?" she asked a little desperately.

"I don't know. I'm not going to let him go, if that's what you're getting at. He led the James River raid, attacked the wagon train Nate Stall was guiding. Thirty-one people were killed. Women and children among them."

Fox Fight made a small disgusted noise. Ruff glanced that way. He couldn't make out the Cheyenne's expression in the darkness.

"I killed no one. One man, maybe. My order was to kill no women, no children."

"What happened? You don't seem to have much control over your people."

"Snake—Snake wants to be war leader. He told his warriors to disobey me."

"It makes a good story."

"It is true!"

Marcia Dawkens was ready to believe it anyway. "He's telling the truth, Justice. I can *feel* it."

"Maybe." Justice had kind of given up on trying to "feel" the truth in a world peopled with liars of all kinds. "Remember this man had plans to attack the wagon train you were with. You could have been killed, or your sister. Any of your friends, like Carrie Dean."

Fox Fight repeated the small disparaging sound. "I did not want this wagon train, Justice. There were too many soldiers. I followed this train for a long while. From the James River. Then it went to Lincoln and I took my people to the mountains."

"And attacked it out here."

"*Snake* attacked it! I did not wish to fight horse soldiers, I told you that. It is too dangerous. Snake is mad. He fights without consideration."

Justice shook his head. How much of that could you believe? As much as you wanted. Marcia soaked it all up, Justice let most of it run off his back. The man wanted to get free and he'd found a soft touch in Marcia Dawkens.

"I saw you," Fox Fight said, "a long way back, yellow-haired woman. Alone in the night. I saw you and I remembered my dream that one day a woman like you would come with me to the mountains. A yellow-haired woman, and I knew I would have you. I followed the wagon train for many miles, many miles, watching for you."

Ruff thought that Fox Fight was laying it on a little

heavy now, but a glance at the starlit face of Marcia Dawkens showed him that she was thirsty for that kind of talk, that she was going to believe anything he said without reservations. Well, why not? She had always been in her sister's shadow. If Fox Fight had been a Philadelphia banker in a top hat, he couldn't have pleased her any more than he did with his short speech. Ruff was getting a little embarrassed riding with them.

Maybe they'd forgotten that Fox Fight was a federal prisoner now, that he was likely going to be executed. And Ruff Justice, who wasn't so easily swayed as Marcia Dawkens, wasn't about to turn him loose.

The coyotes started howling behind them again and they fell silent, quickening their pace.

The land started to fall off steeply and the shifting clouds covered what starlight there was. They rode silently through the trees, feeling their way. Twice they rode out onto a headland from which there was no way down. Far below they could see a red winking eye that might have been the chimney at Walker's Pass or a campfire nearby. They couldn't be sure.

Ruff found the narrow canyon he had seen earlier nearly by chance. It was screened by trees and brush, difficult to find from above, nearly impossible to discover down this low. The horses broke through the wall of brush and they started down. There was mud underfoot and the going was slow. The hills were heavy with the scent of sagebrush and pines. Ruff had Marcia up behind him. Fox Fight was beside them on the paint pony.

He was beside them and then he wasn't. The pony missed its footing and went down, its protesting whickering filling the air. Marcia screamed involuntarily. Ruff leapt from his horse.

The pony had rolled, just missing Fox Fight, and then gone off into the deeper, vast darkness of the gorge below. They could hear rocks sliding and then nothing. They never knew what had happened to the horse.

Ruff pulled Fox Fight to his feet and the Indian grunted with pain.

"What's the matter?"

"Foot. My foot hurts."

"Bad?"

"Broken maybe. Horse got it, I think."

"Ruff—" Marcia began.

Justice cut her off. "Quiet!"

They listened, standing together in the darkness. Upslope they could hear it now. Horses' hooves striking stone, the muffled sound of conversation, which the wind distorted and smothered.

Ruff had his rifle in his hand. He shoved it hard against Fox Fight's ribs, but the Indian didn't look ready to cry out. Maybe he had been telling the truth. Maybe Snake wanted him dead.

Hell, maybe he loved the yellow-haired woman with the twisted face.

Marcia had let the other horse's reins go and it had walked off a way into some head-high sage and oak. Now the three of them got slowly, quietly down, staring up the slope, listening, watching to see if death was going to come rolling down that hillside.

Fox Fight was beside Marcia Dawkens and her hand was on his back. On the other side Justice had his big Spencer against the Indian's side still, being enough of a cynic to trust more to powder and lead than to the power of love.

It seemed that the night had had time to pass a dozen times, that eternity had been compressed and jammed into this one long, endlessly elastic night. Ruff's head thrummed. The rocks beneath him cut his body. His hand was cramped around the rifle he held.

Finally Fox Fight said, "They are gone." He started to rise but Justice nudged him down again. Maybe they were gone. Maybe it was better to wait a few minutes longer after all that time.

The sky at their backs was graying when Justice finally rose stiffly and helped the others up after him. The wind was cold, but the clouds overhead seemed to have dried up. Dawn was coming and the Cheyenne were gone. All things considered, it could have been a hell of a lot worse.

"Come on," Ruff Justice said.

"To the stage stop?" Marcia asked.

"That's right."

"They'll tear him apart down there."

"Could be."

"Haven't you got any mercy in you? Last night he could have called out and gotten us killed!"

"Come on," Ruff repeated, ignoring the woman. You can't argue with a female in love.

He got the horse from out of the dense brush and led it as he walked down the long slope, his rifle in the crook of his arm, Marcia and a silent Fox Fight before him.

Dawn sparked briefly against the gray skies in a violet and orange display and then fizzled. The long plains were in shadow. Smoke rose from the stone chimney of the stage station.

"One more dawn," Ruff Justice said. Tomorrow would be Billy Sondberg's last. He had failed the kid, failed the colonel and Mack Pierce, failed Mary Sondberg. No one could have actually expected much success, but it still rankled.

"They're there," Marcia said softly but with obvious relief. She was pointing toward the stage stop and the surrounding oaks. Now they could see the white tops of the wagons among the trees. There were eleven of them left.

Now Ruff could also see sentries in uniform walking

their patrols. He felt relief loosen his knotted muscles. Maybe things weren't all that safe at Walker's Pass, but it beat the hell out of crawling around a dark mountain with a bunch of renegades looking for you.

Fox Fight had begun to tense, his eyes a little wider, his nostrils flaring. His limp came and went. That foot wasn't that bad.

"Don't try it," Ruff Justice warned him. "I'll shoot you if you make a run for it."

"Justice . . ." Marcia grabbed at his arm, but Ruff shook her off.

"Despite the woman, I'll shoot you, you understand that, Fox Fight?"

"I understand it, Ruff Justice. How could it be otherwise?" Then Fox Fight started on toward the stage station on his own and Ruff followed, calling loudly to the camp, very loudly so that some jumpy soldier didn't put a round in their direction.

"Hey! We're coming in. Hold your fire!"

"Who the hell are . . . Mister Justice!"

"It's me."

"Well, Jesus . . . the woman with you?"

"That's right."

"I'll get the lieutenant."

By the time Ruff reached the oaks, the trees were swarming with people—Updike, Sears Maxwell, Dan Dean and his daughter, Reb Saunders and five soldiers, Lieutenant Sharpe coming on the double, and Ruth Dawkens rushing to Justice to leap into his arms and give him a wet welcoming kiss.

"You bastard," she kept saying, and then she began crying, going to her sister to hug her long and hard while Sharpe tried to sort things out.

"What's happening, Justice?"

"Just what you see. Got lucky and pulled the woman out."

"Who's the prisoner?"

Ruff hesitated. They just might tear him apart if he spoke that name. People had died, and not long ago, because of Fox Fight—or Snake—to these people there would be no distinction and they wouldn't sit around listening to an explanation.

"Just someone I picked up—we'd better talk in private."

Sharpe's eyes clouded. "All right. In the stage station. I've taken over one room as a headquarters."

"Cash Williams still here?"

"Yes. What's he got against Updike?" the lieutenant asked.

"You'd have to ask Cash."

Reb Saunders was walking with them, guarding Fox Fight. Ruth was catching up, lifting her skirts, running to them. Ruff wrapped an arm around her as she arrived, breathless, flushed.

"Marcia told me . . ." she panted. "Has she lost her mind?"

Ruff shushed her as other eyes glanced their way. Reaching the stage stop, they went on in, tramping past the stranded stage-line passengers who gawked and muttered imprecations as the Cheyenne warrior limped past them. Cash Williams caught Ruff's eye and followed. In the back room, usually a storeroom, they shut the door and convened a short meeting.

"All right, what is this?" the lieutenant asked.

"This is Fox Fight," Ruff said. He might as well have dropped a bomb. Sharpe practically leapt at him. Cash Williams, normally placid, went stiff as a board and started sputtering something unintelligible.

Fox Fight looked supremely disinterested in all of it. He sat on a cornmeal sack in the corner, his eyes closed, his bandaged head leaning against the wall.

"That's really him, Mister Justice?" Reb asked. There

119

was a touch of awe in the corporal's voice, experienced as Reb was.

"Afraid so."

"What do we do with him?" Cash Williams asked.

"That's Lieutenant Sharpe's problem," Ruff replied. "I'm turning him over to army custody as of now."

"Those people out there . . ." Sharpe began.

"Yeah. I thought it might be a good idea to keep his identity a secret, if possible. It's bad enough that they know he's Cheyenne. Maybe you could cook up a story, tell them that he's an army scout, I don't know."

"That's an idea. What about his people, Justice?" Sharpe wanted to know. "If they know he's here . . ."

"I imagine they know he's here now, but that won't bring them any faster. They also know we're here with wagonloads of goodies. Fox Fight, believe it or not, seemed to have been some kind of moderating influence on the renegades. Their new leader is a man called Snake, and he doesn't know the meaning of caution."

Cash Williams spoke up again. "You mean you think they'll try to hit the stage stop now? With all the people we've got in here? That's plenty of guns, Justice."

"We haven't got enough to keep him from trying it. For myself I'm going to dry my guns and find some more ammunition. He'll come."

"Kill all the whites," Fox Fight muttered from the corner. Slowly they turned their heads toward him. His dark eyes opened suddenly. "Snake believes that war means to kill all the whites that walk upon this land. He will come. He has made his boasts, he must come."

"I ought to kill you out of hand, you bastard," Sharpe said, but it was said under his breath, and perhaps Justice was the only one who heard him. Ruff glanced sharply at the officer. Aloud Sharpe said, "Corporal Saunders, find Sergeant Walters and send him to me. I want to tighten up our defensive posture. What do you think about using the wagons for barricades, Justice?"

"It wouldn't be a bad idea, but Updike isn't going to go for it. Wrecking the wagons will be the last thing he'll want."

"I wasn't thinking of asking Updike what he wanted," Sharpe said rigidly.

There wasn't much Justice could say to that. He was there to give advice if asked. He had given it. He was growing tired now, very tired. The long miles, the long hours had piled up on him and he was beat. His leg still hurt, his head still rang. He felt like Fox Fight looked, and that was bad. Still, the Indian appeared to be sleeping and that was what Ruff intended to do—after he took care of another little piece of business.

Maybe there was still hope for Billy Sondberg. After all, he had until dawn tomorrow. Ruff shook his head with bitterness. He could try. He couldn't make the clock run backward.

Marcia Dawkens burst in the door and stood with wild, accusing eyes, staring at them all.

"What are you doing to him?" she demanded.

"Nothing at all," Ruff said.

After a moment's confusion Sharpe asked, "What do you want here, Miss Dawkens?"

"Want? I want to see that the prisoner is tended to, that his wounds are treated, that he's fed . . . What's the matter with you, what are you looking at? Are you all mad?"

Sharpe looked at Ruff, who tried to keep his face expressionless. "Do what you must, Miss Dawkens," Sharpe said in the end, "but be careful. A guard will be in this room at all times, but Fox Fight is still a dangerous man. And, I warn you, any attempt to aid him beyond mercy will be dealt with harshly."

Ruth had her temper up now. "What do you think

she's going to do, slip him a gun from her skirts?" Ruth looked to Justice for support but didn't get it. The idea didn't seem so farfetched to him.

They watched for a moment as Marcia went to the injured Indian and started unwrapping the bandage from his head, then Ruff took Ruth by the waist and said, "Come on."

They went out of the storeroom to find a milling crowd. Dan Dean approached Justice, his fists bunched as if to strike. "What the hell's going on in there?"

"You'd have to ask the lieutenant," Justice answered.

Updike was there as well and demanded, "Who's that Indian?"

Again Ruff answered, "Ask the lieutenant."

"You brought him in, didn't you?" Updike said belligerently.

Ruff didn't even respond. He guided Ruth through the crowd of settlers and stage-line customers and out into the fresh, cool air. He stood for a moment looking across the plains to the hills. Would they come from that side? Maybe from all sides at once—that was dangerous because of the oaks, which would be hard to manage on horseback. Let Sharpe worry about it . . . Ruff found that his mind wasn't working too clearly. All of his thoughts were fuzzed at the edges.

"All right?" Ruth asked with concern.

"Sure." He slipped his hands around her waist and drew her nearer, kissing her on the tip of her nose. "When the Cheyenne come, I want you in the stage station too. It'll be awfully crowded, but it'll still be better than the wagons. Likely Sharpe will have his soldiers out here, behind barricades, the civilians inside."

"Where will you be?" Ruth asked. Her eyes were moist and sparkling as she looked up at him.

"As near to you as possible," he promised. "You happen to know anyone who carries a Spencer rifle?"

"Joe McWhorter does. Why?"

"I'd appreciate it if you'd find out if he's got any spare ammunition. I'm awful low. Also I'll need some forty-four-forties for my handgun, but they should be easy to come by."

"All right," she agreed, "but what will you be doing?"

"I've got some people to talk to," Ruff said. "Some people that might know something about a murder."

12

Corporal Reb Saunders had run the message to Sergeant Walters and was now making an ammunition count. Justice found him just as he was finishing up, and he waited patiently, leaning against a grand old oak that had someone's initials carved in it—probably a bored stage passenger, long gone, no longer remembered.

Reb stood up from the ammunition sack and stretched the small of his back. "Hello, Mister Justice. I thought you'd be sleeping by now. You look like you need it."

"I intend to do just that as soon as possible. I need to ask you a question or two, Reb."

"Well, I'm kind of busy," the Texan said, "but if it won't take long."

"I promise it won't."

"Sure."

The two men walked into the oaks a way until Ruff stopped and asked, "That fight you had with Dan Dean—what was that about exactly?"

Reb looked puzzled and slightly annoyed. "It wasn't about a damn thing," he snapped. "The old fool is so jealous of his daughter that he thinks every man that nods to her is up to no good. I stopped to talk to Carrie

Dean for a minute—she really looked forlorn, you know. She'd been crying, crying hard. I tried to cheer her up a little. Dean found us and—hell, I don't know what he thought. He started swinging."

"That was all there was to it?"

Reb was a little incensed. "That was it. Don't you believe me, Ruff?"

"Yes, I do. I had the same experience with the man. He's half-crazy. But was there someone? Is there someone that Carrie Dean liked more than a little?"

"I don't get you."

"Does she have a soldier boyfriend?"

"Not that I know of. If she does, they're closemouthed about it. With reason."

"With good reason," Ruff agreed.

"Why are you asking all this?" It seemed an odd series of questions, and there were more important things in the air, like Snake and his armed renegades getting ready to swoop down on the station.

"Was Carrie Dean Billy Sondberg's girlfriend?"

"Carrie Dean and Billy?" Reb shrugged. "I don't know, Ruff. I never knew the kid that well. He'd of had no reason to tell me, anyway."

"Who would know?"

"Maybe a few of Billy's close buddies. And Carrie herself."

"I don't really want to talk to Carrie. Who knew Sondberg best?"

Reb thought for a moment. "Maybe Ben Price. You know him? He's the buck-toothed kid. He's standing watch near the well over there."

"Thanks, Reb, that's all."

"Ruff, does any of this mean anything? Are you onto something that could clear Sondberg?"

"I don't know. I hope so, but I was never cut out to be a Pink."

No, that was true. He was no detective, but he just

might have hit on an idea. He was fairly sure he had, but he wanted to be surer.

Ben Price was lounging a little more than he should have been against the stone well behind the stage station.

"You're Ben Price, aren't you?"

"That's right, Mister Justice." Price straightened up a little, looking around. "Something wrong?"

"No Indian trouble, no. Listen, Price—it's about Billy Sondberg."

"Yeah, poor Billy." Price added, "He didn't do it, you know."

"You sure?"

"He wasn't that way with women. He was never rough."

"And he had a girlfriend."

"I didn't say that," Price said, recoiling a little.

"But he did."

Price eyed Ruff carefully. "Who says?" he asked with suspicion.

"It's pretty common knowledge," Ruff lied.

Price let out his breath. Then he grinned boyishly. "I thought I was the only one that knew, and I'd promised not to tell."

"It would have meant big trouble."

"I'll say—old man Dean would've ripped him—" Price got suddenly wary. "I promised not to tell."

"Come on, Price, it's too late to hurt anyone. I just need to know about it, that's all."

Price simply turned away and started walking his rounds, his implacable back telling Ruff plainly that no more information was to be forthcoming.

It would have to be Carrie Dean then, as much as Ruff hated to face the girl down. He walked across the camp, looking at the worried faces, the hands gripping rifles and shotguns, the half-aware children playing at their games, looking up with wide eyes.

Sears Maxwell was standing in the mottled shade of

an oak, staring skyward as if looking for his murdered daughter in the heavenly spheres.

"Have you seen Dan Dean?" Ruff asked him.

It took Sears some time to come down from the clouds. "What? Yeah, he's in the stage station still."

"Which one's his wagon?"

"You can't see it. It's next to last in line beyond the trees, but I told you he's not there."

"I know. Thanks."

Ruff walked off, a puzzled Sears Maxwell watching him. The girl wasn't at the wagon, but Ruff found her. She was down near the stream, watching the water run. Distantly, thunder boomed. Tears ran from the girl's eyes. The wind was soft in the willows. Ruff crouched down in front of her, and the red, crying eyes looked up at him.

"What is it?"

"You remember me, Carrie?"

"Yes," she sniffed. "Ruff Justice."

"Do you know what I'm doing here?"

"Yes, you're a scout."

"Yes. But I'm doing a little more than that. I'm looking into the murder of Katie Maxwell."

"Oh." The voice was tiny, distant. Behind Ruff the stream whispered past. "I thought that was over."

"Only if we let it be."

"What do you mean, Mister Justice?"

"Billy Sondberg didn't rape and murder that girl."

"I know it! Billy's such a fine man . . ." The small dark girl seemed to withdraw into herself after a moment's fire.

Ruff lifted her chin. "You know it because he was with you when the murder was supposed to be done."

Her mouth fell open. Cold fury filled her eyes for an instant and Ruff thought some demon inside her was going to come uncoiled. Instead, she just nodded her head slowly.

"He was with you, making love to you, when Katie Maxwell was killed."

"Yes."

"He wouldn't tell anyone that because it meant he wasn't at his post. It also meant that your father would have beaten you half to death if he'd found out you had a boyfriend."

"Yes!" She leaned forward intently, her hands clenching a small handkerchief. She spoke freely suddenly, as if Ruff had unlocked it all. "Father was always afraid I was going to run away like Mother. He hates women, I think. He wouldn't let me go to a school that had boys in it. He won't let me talk to them, be with them at all.

"Then I met Billy and he was everything I wanted a man to be. Kind, good-looking, polite, good-humored . . . he wanted to marry me, but I was afraid to let him ask my father. He would have killed Billy. Literally killed him. We were going to wait until we got to Bear Creek—or maybe even do it at Fort Lincoln."

"You were going to leave your father and marry Billy?"

"Yes. That's it. But in the meantime, we were together, you see, and if my father had known . . ."

"And you were together the night Katie Maxwell was attacked."

"Yes."

"Making love."

"Yes," she said, looking at the ground.

"And Billy Sondberg would rather go to his death than have you shamed or beaten by your father."

"Yes," she said softly.

"And you would let him do it?" Ruff Justice said with some anger.

"He made me promise, don't you see! He made me vow not to say anything about it. He said that it wouldn't be enough anyway, that they wouldn't take my word for it . . . a woman in love with him."

No. Ruff shook his head. No, maybe it wouldn't have been enough to sway the court-martial. Ruff believed her, though. He believed now that Billy Sondberg was innocent, and he admired the kid for his chivalry—it wasn't real smart, but it had been well-intentioned. Dean was just crazy enough to actually have killed his own daughter.

Or someone else's daughter, if he thought she was Carrie?

No telling. Ruff rose, realizing that he hadn't brought Billy Sondberg any closer to exoneration. He knew that Sondberg hadn't done it, but he couldn't prove it. He had a confused girl's word for it that Sondberg had been with her at the time of death. He didn't have the murderer.

And just then he couldn't even make a good guess at who it was. His mind was filled with cobwebs. The weariness had become a palpable weight across his shoulders. He said good day to the Dean girl and dragged himself back to the camp, where he crawled up under a wagon and slept, rifle in hand.

How long he slept he didn't know. It wasn't long enough. Justice woke up with a dry mouth, swollen tongue, encrusted eyes, his blood slowed to a standstill, and he lay there staring at a wagon wheel until his eyes finally focused. And when they did focus, he saw a familiar, pretty face looking at him.

"Hello, Ruth," he said hazily.

She was on her knees, hands on her lap, staring at him. "I didn't mean to wake you up."

"I don't know what woke me up," he said. Unless it was the dream, the one where Fox Fight and Dan Dean had scalped and roasted Billy Sondberg and Carrie as the minister who had a red beard like Caleb Updike's read the wedding ceremony.

"What's happening?" he asked, rolling from under the wagon.

"Everything's quiet. Do you want to eat?"

"I do. You." Ruff kissed her hungrily.

"Not a bad idea. Wrong time."

"Is it?"

"I'm tempted. Do you always wake up this way?" she asked.

"Always."

"Good." She stepped back and Ruff got to his feet. She slipped him a little chamois sack. Ruff peered in at the brass cartridges. A green box of .44s was handed over next. "Am I a good girl?" she asked in a little-girl voice.

"The best!"

"Come on, tall man, I'll feed you. Are you hurt?" She was looking at Ruff's leg. He was limping slightly, but he had thought it didn't show.

"I got shot a few days ago. A present from my old friend, Tandy Monroe."

"A few days ago! And you haven't done anything for it, Ruffin?"

"There wasn't much to do with," he answered.

"You are insane, Mister Justice. Really. Here—this is the Gordons' wagon. I'm traveling with them now. That is, I was. Nobody seems to know if we'll ever travel on now. The Gordons aren't here. They're at the stage station like everyone else, trying to get a peek at Fox Fight."

"Fox Fight! Dammit, I told them not to tell people who he was."

"Word got out. Get up on that tailgate. I'll serve you some food. You could use some."

Ruff barely heard that. Anger surged through his mind, bringing him alert. Nothing but trouble could eventuate from letting Fox Fight's identity get out. He had warned them all, but someone had had too big a mouth.

"Here."

Ruth had been trying to force a bowl of stew on him for some time, he realized suddenly. He took it and honored her with a crooked smile. "Sorry. Is your sister still in there with him?"

"No. She would have stayed, but she couldn't keep her eyes open any longer either. She's in the wagon asleep."

"Good."

"You expect trouble?"

"Yes, I expect trouble."

The stew was good enough, but Justice didn't taste it. He was angry about the Fox Fight business, disturbed by Billy Sondberg's trouble. He told Ruth about his talk with Carrie Dean.

"Poor kid," she said. "That girl's going through an awful time."

"Yeah, almost as bad as Billy Sondberg's."

"You know what I mean—damn that Dan Dean. What's the matter with him? Does he think that by keeping his daughter back he's holding on to his wife?"

Ruff didn't know what Dan Dean thought. Likely he didn't think anything. He just acted. And by acting without thinking, he had precipitated events that had landed Billy Sondberg in the death house.

"If we get out of this," Ruth swore, "I'm taking the girl away from Dan Dean myself. She can work with Marcia and me in our dress shop in Bear Creek."

Ruff didn't answer and Ruth's angry expression faded as she realized that their chances of getting to Bear Creek were very slim now. "It's a nice thought," he said.

"Who did it, Ruff? Who murdered Katie Maxwell?"

"I still don't know. The list of suspects is too long. I have an idea, a crazy idea, but I haven't got anything to substantiate it with."

"All right . . . if you won't tell me. I think—"

She was interrupted by the shot. Ruff grabbed his

rifle and was off in his long-striding run. The settlers and soldiers were rushing for their posts, thinking the Indian attack had begun. Ruff knew it hadn't. Not yet.

The shot had come from the stage stop, and as Ruff reached the front door, he could smell powder smoke. Men surged toward the door of the storeroom where Fox Fight was being kept. Ruff angrily shoved his way through the mob, bursting into the room.

"What happened?"

Fox Fight was all right. He was sitting up, a sneer on his lips. Sharpe wasn't there, nor was the guard, who arrived hastily a moment later, tucking his shirt in.

He goggled at Ruff. "Jesus, I . . ."

Sharpe shoved his way into the room, Cash Williams and Reb Saunders on his heels. Half a dozen other men tried to crowd into the room, but Williams and Saunders shut the door in their faces.

"What in the bloody hell happened?" Sharpe demanded.

The soldier looked ready to come apart. "I had to step outside, sir. I locked him in . . . I didn't figure anything could happen in five minutes."

"You'll do guardhouse time for this," Sharpe said furiously. He was outraged, seemed to take the soldier's inefficiency personally.

Ruff asked Fox Fight. "Was there someone in here? Who tried to shoot you?"

The renegade shrugged. He lifted a pointing finger toward the high, narrow window. "Through there."

"Did you see anyone?"

"No one. No matter. They will come and kill me soon." There was something in Fox Fight's eyes that told Ruff the man was lying. He had seen who tried to kill him and he wasn't talking.

"Fox Fight!" Marcia Dawkens, wild-eyed and frantic, appeared and there was no pretense in her this time as she simply threw herself into the Indian's arms. Sharpe, muttering an angry curse, turned away.

"Let's see what we can find outside," Ruff suggested.

"All right," Sharpe said. "Corporal Saunders, you're in personal charge of this prisoner. Stay in here with him."

"Yes, sir," Reb said. He flicked a salute at Sharpe, who was still scowling angrily at the floor. The guilty trooper was trying to fade into the wall.

"Outside," Sharpe said, and he went out, shoving people back. Justice and Cash Williams were on his heels. Cash shot Ruff one questioning glance, but Justice only shook his head.

Sharpe called out to a soldier to follow him and the four men made their way out the side door of the stage stop. Around the back they found a barrel tipped over beneath the window of the storeroom. The ground beneath was very muddy, the tracks left there large and smeared.

"Only thing I can read is that it was a man wearing boots," Cash Williams offered.

So were they all. And all of them had mud on their boots. They spent a fruitless minute or two looking for a cartridge casing. Ruff got up on the barrel and determined that any man of average height could see in well enough to take a shot at Fox Fight.

He leapt down and shook his head. "There's nothing to be learned here. Tell me, who let the word leak out that it was Fox Fight we're holding?"

"I wish I knew," Sharpe said angrily.

Cash Williams shrugged. "Think someone cared who he was, Ruff? Maybe they just knew he was Cheyenne and wanted to have revenge."

"I don't know," Justice said, although in his own mind he felt fairly sure that he did know what was happening now. But there was no proof! Not enough to free Billy Sondberg.

Sharpe left the soldier standing guard beneath the window and they walked back inside the stage station, where a group of settlers and stage passengers stood waiting.

Ruff looked them over. He'd seen mobs like this before. It was, pure and simple, a lynch mob. They'd chosen Caleb Updike for their spokesman.

"We want the Indian, Lieutenant Sharpe."

"You can't have him. He's my prisoner."

"He's Fox Fight, isn't he? Chief of the renegades. The bastard that led the raid on us?"

"He's Fox Fight."

"He's living," an older man put in, "while my wife's lyin' cold in her grave."

"Things aren't done this way, gentlemen," Sharpe responded. "He's a government prisoner now. Anyone trying to take Fox Fight from my custody will be committing a federal offense. You'll be liable to felony charges—"

"What are we listening to all this chatter for," a voice from the back of the crowd shouted. It was always the ones in the back, Ruff had noted, who wanted action. A half-dozen soldiers with weapons had come up behind Sharpe. The two groups faced each other again as they had back down the trail.

Ruff glanced to his right and saw Marcia Dawkens standing in the partly open storeroom door. Her crooked face was set, the determination Justice saw there giving it a character it hadn't had before. She had been a changed woman since Fox Fight came into her life. He might be a murdering savage, but by God, he was *her* murdering savage.

Sergeant Lew Walters broke things up. He poked his head in the door, his anxious eyes searching for his lieutenant. "They're coming, sir. One of the sentries reports seeing feathers and paint."

13

There was a moment's awed silence and then a mad rush toward the windows and doors. Sharpe was calling out orders, settlers shouted for their women and children. Curses rang through the stage station, and the sound of a grown man crying in fear.

Outside, the soldiers were overturning the settlers' wagons, forming a barricade, and angry shouts went up. Obviously Sharpe hadn't shared that part of his plan with the homesteaders.

"Ruff!"

Ruth rushed in the side door, her shawl around her shoulders, carrying a canteen of water to cool the rifle barrels if necessary, and a sack of provisions in her other hand in case the siege became an extended one—and it had every indication of doing just that.

Snake had come to drive the whites out. The soldiers, the number of white guns meant nothing to him. Nor did the lives of his warriors. He would hurl them against the tiny fortress time and again until there was total victory . . . or total defeat.

"Where's Marcia?" Ruth asked worriedly.

"She's all right. She's in there with Fox Fight. There's a soldier with them."

"Thank God." Then she asked, "I haven't heard any shots yet."

"There haven't been any. A sentry saw Snake a long way off. There's a good field of view from this station." Which was one reason Ruff Justice had chosen this site for the Court sisters when they were building Great Western.

They hadn't heard shots yet, but they would, plenty of them. They could hear Lew Walters bellowing, "Get that goddamned wagon on its side, you slackers! Look out—there's a loose kid. Grab the little son of a bitch, Chambers!"

Then after a time it was silent, eerily silent. Men hunched against the walls, their rifles projecting from the windows. Outside, soldiers stood behind the over-turned wagons, waiting. Ruff was beside the north window, Ruth beside him. Together they watched a lonesome cloud drift past, its shadow flitting across the earth, darkening the station briefly.

Then Justice saw the bit of movement in the oaks and he tensed, nudging Ruth aside slightly.

"Something?" she whispered.

He nodded, and speaking aloud, quietly but in a voice that carried across the station, he said, "I've got some over here. In the oaks. Cash, can you see anything?"

"Not yet. Where?"

"The west end. The big twin oak there."

"No."

"He's behind the tree. Wait—there's another in the grass. See him?"

"O.K. I see that one now."

One of the settlers had rushed to Cash Williams' window and Cash pushed him aside angrily.

"Get to your own post," the stage manager said. Then to Ruff, "Which one's mine, Ruffin?"

"Anything to the left of the smith's shed, all right?"

"All right."

It grew tensely silent. Now and then an impatient thumb hooked the hammer of a rifle and drew it back, the ratcheting loud in the stillness. Ruff was aware of Ruth's close presence. He turned his head and smiled at her before turning his gaze to the oaks.

He had spotted three Cheyenne by now. That probably meant there were a dozen or more in the oaks. He wiped his hand on his buckskin pants and settled in to wait.

"Here they come!" someone on the south side shouted.

Sharpe yelled, "Let the soldiers fire first. Hold your fire!"

It didn't do a lot of good. Fear and anxiety had gripped the men in the stage station. Nightmares and stark panic came alive as the first flesh-and-blood renegade, a war cry filing his mouth, rushed the stage station.

A dozen weapons fired at the Cheyenne, cutting him to ribbons. The soldiers, still armed with those damned old breech-loading Springfield rifles, were at a disadvantage. The old hands were quick at reloading the single-shot rifles, but they couldn't match the firepower of the repeating Winchesters most of the renegades were carrying.

When the next wave of attacking Indians charged out of the oaks, they were plenty of targets for everyone. They came mounted this time, shooting beneath their horses' necks or wildly charging the soldiers behind the wagons, trusting blindly to their leader's good magic.

There wasn't enough good magic to go around. A young warrior went down, and another. A paint pony was hit in the lungs, tumbled head over heels, and crushed its rider. Now from the north side the attack began.

"Ruff!" Ruth gripped Justice's arm and he had to shake her off.

"Get down."

"There's five or six of them!" Ruth was made of good stuff, but she hadn't gone Indian fighting before.

"All right. I've got to let them come in a little. I don't want to chase them all back into the woods. Let them get into the open, see." He spoke quietly, almost to himself, using his voice to soothe Ruth. "See 'em, Cash? One more behind the big rock there. Now he's moving. Taking himself out of cover."

"Ready?" Cash asked. And Cash, who *had* done some Indian fighting, sounded a little nervous himself. From the south side of the stage station the sounds of fighting had intensified. Gunshots rang out continuously, and the cries of pain had begun to fill the little building. Richochets whined angrily off the stone walls. Ruff looked at Cash Williams and nodded.

Cash fired almost immediately. Ruff couldn't see if it was a hit or not. His own first target had decided to be bold, and he charged the station, firing his Winchester wildly, from the hip. The renegade was dressed in cavalry pants and breechclout, wearing only crimson paint above the waist.

Ruff Justice settled in behind the sights, drew back the hammer of the Spencer, and cursing under his breath, squeezed off. The .56 had a kick like a mule. The renegade was flung backward like a charging dog reaching the end of its tether. Ruff cursed again and Ruth looked at him, her forehead furrowed with puzzlement.

Justice fired again, missed as his target veered unexpectedly aside, levered a fresh round in, and squeezed off another shot. The .56 clipped the Indian's arm off at the shoulder and he fell to the earth, spewing blood everywhere, his severed arm still twitching like a thick snake.

Ruff Justice cursed again. His face was intent, angry, his eyes piercing, softly misted. Ruth huddled against the wall, watching. Once she met Cash Williams' eyes as the stage manager reloaded. Her expression caused him to look up at Ruff Justice and he nodded at Ruth as if to say, "Yes, that's the way he is."

It was a complex man Ruth was watching, and she knew suddenly what was happening inside of Justice. He was a killing thing, a hunting man, a rover, and a man of violence—but it was the battle he loved and not the killing, the game of war, not the death it brought. Yet compassion was not going to still his trigger finger. He would kill. He would sorrow for those who must die, but he would kill when and how he had to.

The east side became the focal point of battle suddenly. A cry of alarm went up from the windows on that side. Snake had merely been feinting on the other two sides. Now he threw the bulk of his force against the eastern wall. Snake might be a wild-eyed zealot, but he also knew something about warfare.

Ruff heard the barrage of shots, the peppering of the stone walls with enemy fire, and he turned in time to see an Indian's hand with a pistol clenched in it thrust into a window on the east side.

Reb Saunders was below the window and Justice shouted. Reb thrust his own pistol out and fired blindly. Both guns spewed smoke and lead. Reb's was the luckier shot. The renegade's face that had appeared in the window was blown away in a mask of blood. Reb, visibly shaken, gave the thumbs-up to Ruff, who managed a grin.

"Stay here," Justice told Ruth. "Cash? You got it?" At Cash's nod, Ruff crossed the room in a crouch, stepping over a stage passenger who had taken a bad one low down in the groin and now lay writhing, near death, on the floor.

Ruff settled in beside Reb Saunders and began to put some rounds through the big buffalo gun.

The .56 spoke its magic again and again as Justice

picked a renegade from his charging pony's back, then put a lucky round through the skull of a fleeing renegade. That one had been toting a soldier's scalp with him.

The barricade on that side had broken down. Two of the wagons were in flames, another was being dragged aside by Indians on horseback despite the fierce fire from the windows of the stage stop and from the soldiers who had retreated to the barricades on the south side. Those who hadn't remained behind, dead and bloody against the dark earth.

A wave of mounted Cheyenne appeared from out of the trees and poured through the gap in the burning barricade. Ruff fired his Spencer until it was empty, then drew his Colt—there simply wasn't time to reload. They were driven back by continuous fire, but three more settlers had been shot. The wounded now littered the floor of the station, their groans horrible, chilling.

"Goddamn fools won't keep their heads down," a man beside Ruff Justice said. Then he stood and took a bullet through the neck. He toppled to the floor beside Justice, dead.

It was so still suddenly that they could hear nothing but the moaning of the wounded, the crackling of the flames as the wagons burned.

"Where'd they go?"

"Did we chase 'em off?"

Justice could see little through the smoke on the east side now. He scooted away from the window and went to where Ruth was trying to bandage an injured man. It was high on the thigh and the big artery was cut. He didn't have a chance, and Ruth must have known it.

"Is it over?" the dying man asked. "Did we win?"

"It's over," Ruff Justice lied. "We whipped 'em."

A slight smile flickered across the settler's mouth and then he was dead.

"That's my wagon," Caleb Updike roared like a

wounded cougar. He rushed toward the door and they had to hold him back. He knocked two men down before they wrapped him up. He struggled in their arms and kicked out blindly. "That's my wagon that's on fire. My wagon!"

"Too late to put it out now, Updike. You can replace whatever you've lost."

Ruff Justice knew he couldn't. He just couldn't replace the embezzled bank funds that were burning up in his wagon. Caleb Updike was back where he started from, broke and alone. Someone would have to write the miners of Leadville and tell them that Updike didn't quite get away with it.

"Mister Justice?"

It was Marcia Dawkens. She looked pale, small, frightened.

"What is it?"

"Please. Will you talk to Fox Fight? There's something he's told me—well, you should hear it. Someone should."

"All right." Ruff got to his feet and started toward the storeroom. The young soldier standing guard inside looked stony, confused, and angry.

Fox Fight was still crouched in the corner. "How is the battle going?" he wanted to know.

"A lot of casualties. Both sides."

"Snake will never quit."

"I know that." Ruff stood over the Indian. "The lady says you had something to tell me."

"Yes. Something you need to know. The man who tried to shoot me through the window—I was lying when I said I did not see him. I know who it was."

"Who?" Behind Ruff the sounds of fighting had died away, but there was an intense, busy hum as people prepared to fight, to die.

"First I must tell you why," Fox Fight said.

"There isn't much time before Snake returns."

"There is time enough. Listen to me, Ruff Justice. I told you that I followed this wagon train for a long time—from the James River—but I did not attack it because of the soldier guards."

"Yes, I recall that," Ruff said.

"I told you also that I fell in love with a yellow-haired woman . . ." He looked at Marcia, who flushed—with pride, Ruff Justice thought. "And since I was in love I took a risk one night."

"What kind of risk?"

Someone else had eased into the room, but Ruff paid no attention to him. Fox Fight hesitated, licked his dry lips, and went on. "I wanted to see the yellow-haired woman and so I came into the white camp one night."

"You what?" Marcia interjected.

"I wanted to see you, and so alone in the dark of night I crept to the wagons to see if I could find you."

"A mighty big risk," Ruff said.

Fox Fight shrugged. "Many times I have done similar things. I have taken the gun from a sleeping man's holster . . . but on this night I was unlucky. I did not see the yellow-haired woman. Instead, I saw a murder."

"You what?" Marcia gasped.

"I saw a murder, Ruff Justice. A young woman. I saw her raped by a man and she lay there crying, threatening to kill him, to tell everyone so that they would hang him. He told her to shut up. He said she had teased him. It was her fault."

"What happened then?" Ruff's voice had gone cold. He had been holding his breath without realizing it.

"He killed her. Maybe, I think, I could have stopped it, but it was very quick. It would have cost my own life anyway. It was very bad. I waited while the man stood up and looked around and wiped his hair back. Then he sneaked away and so did I."

"The man . . . who was it, Fox Fight?" Ruff Justice asked.

"Him." Fox Fight pointed toward the door. "He must

have known I was there somehow. And so he tried to kill me. It was him that murdered the girl. I saw this. It was Lieutenant Sharpe."

"He's a liar!"

Sharpe was in the doorway, his face livid, his mouth drawn down, his body trembling. "He's a lying Indian bastard! I didn't do it. Billy Sondberg did. Everyone knows that."

"Billy Sondberg wasn't even there," Justice said coldly. "It was hours later that he found the body and sat there in shock waiting to be discovered, knowing that it had happened on his post. You knew that Sondberg was absent from his post, didn't you, Sharpe? You made your rounds and found him gone. And so you used his absence to rape the Maxwell girl . . ."

"No!" Sharpe had drawn his service revolver. He stood, chest rising and falling as he faced Justice, the guard, and Fox Fight. "You'll not put me up before a wall. The little bitch deserved all she got. She was a teasing little thing. Then she pretended she didn't want it. I had to do it. If you could only understand . . . It took me a long damn time to get these lieutenant's bars. She wanted to wreck my career before it got started. And then—what luck!—this damned Indian had to be there. I saw him. I didn't know his name, but I knew he was there. No matter. I knew he'd take off. I'd never see him again. And then he turned up here!"

"You let Sondberg take the blame."

"Why not? He was off screwing that Dean girl instead of watching his post. Dereliction of duty!" Sharpe was getting a little wild-eyed now. "It was chance that let him find the girl, stay with her through the rest of the night until we could arrest him. You see, I'm shot through with good luck. I always have been. Except for that stinking Indian being there. That's the only thing that tripped me up!"

The door behind Sharpe opened and Cash Williams

blundered in. The officer turned that way and Ruff leapt.

He hit Sharpe low, his hand clawing for the revolver, which went off just over Ruff's ear, sending a deadly, jagged ricochet whining around the room as Ruff and Sharpe hit the floor hard.

Sharpe had the strength of a madman. He fought back wildly with both fists, landing punches on Ruff's ears, throat, face, but it wasn't enough. Justice caught him with a short chopping right that put Sharpe out; the officer stayed down as Ruff rose, panting.

"You filthy son of a bitch," Ruff Justice said quietly. Then he looked to the wide-eyed guard. "You'd better get Sergeant Walters, son."

The guard had taken one step when the thunder guns began to fire outside the station and the Cheyenne came in again.

14

Walters was shaken. He was a good soldier, but he didn't know how to handle the arrest of a superior. He was reluctant to do anything until Ruff repeated almost word for word the confession and Marcia and the guard swore that it was true.

"I got an Indian war to worry about," Walters complained.

"All right. Let's take care of Sharpe and then get to it. Arrest him."

Walters still hesitated, but eventually he did it: arrested Sharpe and took over command with three soldiers standing by to witness this event. Outside, the fighting was growing ferocious. Walters glanced that way and said, "Hell, tie him up, men. Let's do the job they pay us for."

Two soldiers were left to watch Sharpe, who spat out a venomous stream of invective as he was tied and dragged to a corner opposite Fox Fight's.

"Ruff," Marcia Dawkens said, taking his arm. "Fox Fight cleared Billy Sondberg. He could have remained silent. Couldn't you—"

"It's not up to me," Ruff answered shortly. He wasn't sure the West needed Fox Fight freed to wander the plains again. Marcia bit at her lip in anger and turned away to go back to her Indian lover.

Outside, more wagons were burning. More dead littered the field, more wounded lay wide-eyed, babbling, against the floor of the stage station. Gunsmoke was heavy in the air, stinging eyes and nostrils. The constant roar of guns was deafening. Ruff found Ruth, paused long enough to give her an encouraging smile, and got back to the fighting.

The renegades attacked like a crazed pack of wolves, throwing their bodies recklessly into the gunfire of the besieged settlers. Snake didn't care how many casualties it cost, apparently. He wanted to win at any price.

The big .56 Spencer Ruff Justice carried spoke again and again until the barrel was hot, until finally the ammunition gave out and he was forced to use the Colt. The renegades surged forward, running over their own dead, again reaching the windows. It was hand-to-hand briefly as three painted, battle-crazed Cheyenne breached the southern defense and clambered in the window.

One took a bullet in the chest, another split a settler's head with his tomahawk before being clubbed down by a rifle. The third came face-to-face with Sears Maxwell, and Maxwell was a match for him with a knife. The Indian severed three of Maxwell's fingers with a stroke of his knife, but Maxwell's bowie ripped the Cheyenne's belly open and he fell to the floor writhing, dying.

And then they were gone again, falling back, whooping, whistling, yelping. Silence came in like a palpable thing; smoke drifted out the windows. The wounded and dying moaned softly.

Ruth was bandaging Sears Maxwell's hand.

"I heard," was all Maxwell said. "Heard it wasn't the kid." The hatred, the anger had gone out of Maxwell's face. Pain was there replacing it, and shame.

"No, it wasn't the kid."

"Feel bad." Maxwell shook his head. He gazed at his damaged, gauze-wrapped hand. "The kid'll die in the mornin', won't he?"

"I suppose so. There's no way to make it back in time," Justice said. "No way at all."

"Maybe the colonel will give him a stay of execution," Ruth said. "Can he do that? Stay it for a day or two, give you time to get back—if the Indians let us?"

"Won't work," Sears Maxwell said. "No stay for the kid."

"What are you talking about?" Justice asked.

"Charity Blaine." Maxwell's sad eyes lifted to meet Ruff Justice's.

"What about Charity Blaine?" He explained to Ruth, "The gunman who worked for Caleb Updike down in Colorado. The one I thought had ridden to the wagon train from here."

"He did. Came in, got paid, left," Sears Maxwell said. "Charity Blaine laughed, said it was the easiest money he'd ever make. Favor to me. Updike did it as a favor to me."

"Did what?" Justice demanded, feeling he already knew.

"I didn't trust the army to execute its own man after we left. I needed to know the man who killed my daughter was going to die. Updike sent Charity Blaine to the fort. If Sondberg don't get shot all legal in the morning, Charity Blaine will do it."

Maxwell just stared at Ruff for a long minute. Then slowly he shook his head. "Either way it's murder, isn't it? If the army hangs the kid, if Blaine does it—it's murder, and I'm the one responsible."

Ruff wanted to say something but there was nothing to say. Momentarily he felt like placing a comforting hand on Sears Maxwell's shoulder, but he couldn't bring himself to do that either, so in the end he just turned away.

147

"Not much left," Reb Saunders said. He had his ammunition sack before him. He handed three cartridges to the soldier on his left, two to the man on his right, and then shook the sack. It was empty. "We're about done, Mister Justice."

"You can't mean they'd come back!" Dan Dean said, his voice breaking. "Not after what we've fed them!" He didn't sound so very tough right then. Carrie Dean was nearby, hands folded, watching her father, feeling who-knew-what emotion.

Ruff made the rounds, peering out each window, seeing the desolation, the burned wagons, the dead. Then he went into the storeroom.

"How does it go now, Justice?" Fox Fight asked.

"You know how it's going. Snake must be insane. Every man and woman on both sides will be dead before he stops."

"I can stop him," Fox Fight said.

Ruff frowned. "What are you talking about?"

"I can stop him. Perhaps I can stop him."

"How?"

"In single combat. I can challenge Snake for the leadership of the tribe. If I kill him, I will be supreme war leader again. Then I will withdraw my people."

"The hell he would," one of the soldiers said. Cash Williams had wandered in to lean against the wall. In the far corner Lieutenant Sharpe sat as if he were in another world, one where none of this had any meaning.

"It is a chance, Ruff Justice," Fox Fight said.

"Your life for our lives."

"Yes. Let me go and I will battle Snake. I vow that I will take away my warriors when it is done."

"If you let him go, he'll just join up with the others, Mister Justice," the soldier objected.

Walters came in and asked what the hell was going on. They told him.

"No," the sergeant said flatly. "You can't trust a man like that."

"We don't have much chance without some help," Cash Williams responded. "You see the ammunition supplies? There ain't any. We've got maybe a dozen able-bodied men left."

"I can't make a decision like this on my own," Sergeant Walters said dismally.

"You'll have to."

"What about the settlers? What about Updike? Let him make the decision."

"Caleb Updike is dead," Cash told the NCO.

"It's in your lap, Walters."

"Mister Justice?" The sergeant looked pleadingly to his scout for help.

"You trust him, don't you, Ruff?" Marcia asked desperately.

"No. No, I don't trust him, but I don't see that we've got anything to lose. If he's being honest, he'll fight Snake hand-to-hand—that'll give us a chance. If he's lying and takes off, well, one more out there isn't going to turn the tide of battle. Likely if we don't try something, there won't be anyone left to hold Fox Fight prisoner anyway. Damned hard to fight without ammunition. I say let him go—there's not much to lose."

"I vote with Ruff," Cash said, "if anyone cares about my vote."

Walters hesitated. "I should talk to the settlers."

"It's an army matter. He's an army prisoner. We're in the middle of a battle."

"Justice . . . aw, hell, they'll probably bust me for this. Let the Indian go!"

Fox Fight watched darkly as Ruff sawed through the ties on his ankles and wrists. "So, you do not trust me, Justice."

Ruff just looked at him. "Should I?"

"I want to go out the window. I am afraid the people out there won't let me go."

"All right. Get going."

Fox Fight turned back to Marcia briefly, touching her yellow hair before he climbed up on a cornmeal barrel and clambered through the high window of the storeroom.

"Well, it's done," Ruff said. "Let's get the word to those out there to hold their fire."

There was an uproar when Justice told them what had been done, but as they realized there was a chance of getting out alive, they quieted. People crowded the windows. It wasn't real safe to do so, but they had to see, had to know.

"They won't do it out in the open, will they?" Sears Maxwell asked.

"No telling. Maybe. Fox Fight might like for us to see it all."

"If he has any intention of doing it at all. Who says we can believe him?"

After a while the questions died down and they stood watching, staring across the empty grass beyond the oaks, past the dead bodies, the slaughtered stock, the burned wagons, toward a distant hope.

"There they are!" Reb Saunders shouted excitedly. The people around Ruff pressed against him, surging toward the window. They could see them now, distantly. Two Indians, tiny figures with copper skin, wearing only breechclouts. The sun glinted on something small and shiny in the hand of one man.

"Knives," Cash Williams said for no reason.

They could see nothing. No facial features stood out at that distance. Both men were similarly built. They seemed to be talking. A hand was raised, and then they came together violently.

"I knew he wouldn't lie. I knew it," Marcia Dawkens cried.

He hadn't lied, but that didn't mean he was going to win. The tiny creatures groped and grappled and performed a miniature ballet of death. There was no sound they could hear, only tiny puffs of dust. They rolled to the ground, rose. They could see nothing of what was happening.

Then one of the two fell and stayed there.

"It's Snake," Reb Saunders whispered.

"No, it's not," Sears Maxwell argued. "The one on the ground—it's Fox Fight. We're sunk."

The Indian who had won turned toward them and then walked away without a gesture. He was suddenly out of view and there was nothing out on the plains but a small inert body.

"Here he comes!" someone cried out, and a rifle was raised.

"Put that damned gun down! Wait, hold your fire."

There was a lone Indian coming in on a painted war pony, a lance held high overhead. No one breathed. They could hear the drumming of hoofbeats now. Dust spumed up behind the pony.

"Fox Fight!"

It was Fox Fight. There was blood on his arm and his hand. He held a war lance high, and as he halted the pony in a whirlwind of dust, he threw the lance, burying the head of it in the earth before the stage station's window.

"Marcia!" Ruth Dawkens yelled, and then Ruff saw her too. She must have climbed out the storeroom window. Now, with her skirts held high, she ran to where Fox Fight waited, and he swung her up behind him on the horse.

"Stop him," Ruth shouted, but there was no way to stop them.

"Maybe it's the right way," Ruff Justice said.

Ruth looked at him, conflicting emotions dueling in

her brown eyes. "Maybe . . ." she said at last. "Maybe it is the right way, the only way. She was never very happy in our world."

Then the horse was running, Marcia clinging to Fox Fight, and after a while they couldn't see them anymore. It was a long ten minutes later that they saw the Cheyenne warriors mass once more, and they tensed, gripping their weapons tightly.

"The bastard," Sears Maxwell said.

"They're leaving," Ruff told him. "He just wanted to show us that they were leaving."

And then they did pull off. The renegade army led by Fox Fight, who rode with his yellow-haired woman, pulled off and left the battered stage station to heal itself.

Ruth was crying, clinging to Justice. Sears Maxwell broke into an impromptu jig. In the corner a woman wailed over the body of her man. A child cried loudly, querulously.

Ruff Justice found Cash Williams in front of the station, surveying the wreckage.

"Have you got a coach intact, Cash?"

"Sure. I think so, at least."

"Will you find out? What about horses?"

"I've got a team, yes." Cash's eyes narrowed. "What have you got in mind, Ruff?"

"Billy Sondberg."

"No one can make it back to Fort Lincoln by dawn. No one."

"Maybe not. But I'm going to try, and I'm going to take Sharpe—and his confession—with me to stop that execution. We'll do it by stage, with fresh horses every fifty miles."

"You'll run those horses into the ground."

"It's worth it, for a kid's life."

Cash wagged his head. "You'll never make it, Ruff, not if you leave now."

"I intend to leave now—or as soon as you get me hitched up."

"Who's driving?" Cash asked.

"Me."

"All night long?"

"I don't have any choice."

Cash grinned. "Sure you do. I'm going with you. I'll get that team buckled in in five minutes flat."

"Ruff?" It was Ruth Dawkens. She'd been listening to the conversation. "I'm going with you, if it won't slow you down."

"What about Bear Creek, the dress shop?"

"Without Marcia that doesn't matter. I'd just as soon return home."

"All right. You're sure? It's going to be a long rough ride."

"If you're going, I'm going."

"So am I." The voice belonged to Carrie Dean. She looked very small, very determined. Her father was watching her from the door of the stage station. "I'm going along too, Mister Justice."

"It might be a bad idea. There's a good chance we won't make it, Carrie."

"I want to know. One way or the other."

"What about him?" Ruff nodded toward Dan Dean, who looked strangely empty.

"I've told him. He knows."

"All right. Get a few things—nothing heavy, no trunks, and climb aboard. I'm getting the prisoner."

He found Sharpe where he had left him. He gazed out at Ruff from the tunnels of his eyes. He seemed to know now that it was all up. Justice led him out, walked him to the stage, and sat him in it, tied feet and hands. It wasn't real comfortable, but that was too bad.

Cash had brought the wheel horse around, and as he

backed it into position, Ruff buckled the harness down, attaching the trace chains while Cash went back for the next animal.

"There's nothing to guarantee Fox Fight won't have a try at us once we get out on the plains," Cash pointed out.

"Nothing at all."

"You think we're finished with them?"

"I don't know, Cash. He gave us his word about the other—from here on, I wouldn't pretend to know what Fox Fight will do. If he's smart, he'll take his people north to Canada, out of the war zone."

"What about the woman? What about Marcia Dawkens?" Cash straightened up. His features were vague in the failing light.

"The woman found something to live for. That's about all anyone can hope to find."

"Yeah," Cash was forced to agree, "I suppose you're right."

The women were back. Ruth looked determined; Carrie Dean slightly bewildered, as if she'd astonished herself with her own strength in breaking away from her father.

"Ready?" Ruff helped them up, kissing Ruth in passing. "Will you be all right with him?" Justice asked, nodding at Sharpe. The officer was trussed up pretty well. He wasn't going anywhere.

"He gives us any trouble and we'll take care of him," Ruth said.

Sharpe's eyes sparked. "I have the idea you mean it . . . and that you're just the ladies to do it," Justice said.

"You bet. Ruff, don't be thinking about us. Get this damned coach into Fort Lincoln by dawn."

"I'm going to try," was all Ruff could say. He swung up beside Cash and as his bottom touched wood, Cash cracked his whip over the ears of the leaders. The coach lurched into motion and they raced out of the smoldering stage station, dodging the rubble and wreckage of battle, the dead and the brokenhearted living.

Fort Lincoln was a hell of a long way off.

15

●●●━━◆━━●●●

Cash knew the trail and he knew the horses. He knew the coach he was driving, but as darkness settled, his wild early pace had to be slowed some. They were racing blindly into the night, the skies purple and deep red behind them.

Even this far out they could smell smoke from the stage-station battle hanging in the air like a distant memory. Cash was intent, using the whip freely. His hat had blown back to hang down his back on its rawhide string. He leaned far forward, urging the horses on. The froth was whipped from their mouths by the wind of motion. Their manes swirled around their necks, their eyes were wide and frantic.

Ruff Justice sat beside Cash grimly holding the rail around the coach box, knowing that whatever they did, no matter how many times Cash cracked that whip, they were liable to be late.

They splashed across Cougar Creek, shallow, wide, silver in the starlight, and rolled up the long grade beyond, weaving through the pines, the horses faltering now. Cash's expression was wooden as he whipped the team on.

"They'll die," he said at one point. "Too much for them, Ruff."

"Hold 'em back a little, Cash."

But Cash shook his head. It was a young soldier or the foundering horses. He laid the whip on them again.

It was full dark when they came rolling down out of the piny hills toward the small grassy valley below. There was a fire going in the fireplace at the Coyote Springs station. As they rolled up, the door was opened, casting a yellow rectangle against the darkness.

"Who's that? Cash!"

"Get a team out, Windy. Move it!"

"Express run?" the old man asked, but he was already moving toward the stable.

An older woman came out of the station, wiping her hands on her apron. She had a Peacemaker belted on around her waist. "Venison stew, folks. Cornbread if you'll let me heat it up."

"No time, Molly," Cash shouted. "Sorry."

The woman shrugged and got to work on the harness along with Ruff and Cash. Windy came on the run with the first fresh horse, clucking his tongue at the sight of the hard-used team.

"Run 'em to the nub, didn't you, Cash?"

"Yes, and I'll run these the same way."

Molly asked, "How's Indian trouble back down the line, Mister Williams?"

"They're quiet right now," Cash said, choosing the easy answer. "Windy, get those horses."

Ruth had gotten down and was trying to help. There were really too many fingers there, but Ruff appreciated the effort. "How's our prisoner doing?" he asked.

"Fine—bouncing around all over hell. Knocked himself silly on a couple of those sharp turns. We decided to keep him on the floor. He makes a good foot cushion."

"Don't take him too lightly," Ruff warned her.

"You ever see this one?" she asked, and from her

skirt came a big Walker Colt, an iron hogleg with the punch of a light cannon.

"You're more dangerous than I thought, woman."

"And how dangerous did you think I was?" she asked teasingly.

"Plenty."

"You were right." She kissed Ruff quickly and stood back as Windy brought in two more horses.

"If I'd a known you were coming through . . ." Windy began, but no one paid any attention, so he let the sentence dwindle to nothing.

"Mister Justice?" Molly had a cardboard box in her hands. "Something for you folks to chew on."

"Thanks."

In another ten minutes they were rolling out, Justice driving. It had been a while since he handled a coach, but it came back. The moon was beginning to rise and they raced beneath its glaring eye out onto the long plains while the wind from the north pushed at them, shoving, bullying the frail coach and its passengers.

The team loosened up and found its pace. Ruff let them run, not bothering with the whip. It was difficult to talk above the wind and the rumbling of the coach, the pounding of the hooves, and so they didn't speak much. They simply stared ahead, willing themselves onward.

The lead horse went down in a heap and the rest of the team piled onto it, swerving different directions, the stage swaying wildly, then hitting a rut and bouncing high into the air. Justice laid on the brake and he and Cash both yanked back on the reins. The coach teetered high up on one wheel and then with a shudder slammed to the ground to land upright, swaying.

"Holy Christ," Cash Williams breathed.

They leapt from the stage. The lead horse had broken a foreleg in a prairie-dog hole. There wasn't anything to do but cut it out and continue.

"Thought you were teaching those animals to fly," Ruth cracked, but there was a nervous edge to her voice.

"If I was, I didn't do much of a job at it."

"We're going to have to slow down, Ruff," Cash said.

Justice looked to the Big Dipper, reading the time. "We can't, Cash."

"We're lucky we didn't wreck the coach that time."

"Cash, we're right on the borderline now between making it and not making it. If we wreck the coach, well, fate's taken a hand. If we fail because we're too cautious, then that's my fault, and I don't want the guilt."

"Hell, drive on then." Cash swung up. "Adrienne Court will know where to send the bill for the coach too."

And knowing her, Ruff thought, she would. He snapped the reins, and the coach jerked into motion. There was one more stage station before Bismarck, but if these horses lasted that far, it would be miraculous. They were short a horse now, and the lead horse at that. Driving them was getting to be work. Ruff's hands were knotted and growing blistered. His arms were heavy, sore.

"Let me have 'em, Ruff," Cash said, and Ruff gratefully handed the leather ribbons over.

Even Cash Williams couldn't make that tired team run any faster, however. Justice sat watching the Big Dipper ever so slowly turn around, its handle like the hand on an immense cosmic clock. It had to be close on to four in the morning when they reached the new station at Big Rock.

Nobody was there.

"Hello the house!" Cash called. He looked at Ruff in the darkness and climbed down.

"Watch yourself, Cash."

"I'd appreciate it if you'd cover me."

"You're covered," Justice said. He knew what Cash felt. They had been through too much in the last few days to buy it now. He watched from the box as Cash approached the apparently deserted stage station. The only sounds were the ragged breathing of the horses, the distant calling of a hunting owl. Cash rapped on the door loudly and then went in, pistol in hand. He was back in a moment.

"Nobody here. Place is cleaned out."

"What do you mean nobody's here!"

"It's not my fault, Ruffin."

"No," Ruff apologized. "Sorry." He wiped the sweat from his eyes and swung down, wrapping the reins around the break handle.

Ruth's head poked out of the stage window. "What's wrong, Ruff?"

"I'm not sure yet. Stay put."

Cash had gone around to the barn. It was empty. "No horses, Ruffin. They must have taken them."

"Scared off, do you think?"

"Maybe. We had a new crew here. Indian stories might have chased them off." Cash sighed. "Now we're done."

"No," Justice said. "Now we've got to find another way."

"Without horses, Ruff . . ."

"How far is Lee Carver's place from here?"

"Carver—five miles on maybe."

"All right. He's got horses."

"That cantankerous old bastard . . ."

"That's what he is, but he likes gold money."

"Are you holding gold money, Ruff?"

"No. The Great Western's IOU is as good as gold now."

"She'll kill me," Cash said, thinking of his boss. "Adrienne Court'll kill me."

"It's our only chance."

"All right." Williams breathed out a little heavily. "Let's see what Lee Carver's like when you wake him from a sound sleep."

He was like a bull that had been cut and treated with kerosene was what he was like, but the old man and two of his sons in nightshirts and jeans hitched up four fresh horses, accepted Cash's IOU, and stood scowling as Ruff hied those ponies out of there.

There couldn't have been an hour before sunrise, and Lincoln was still just too far.

Carver's horses weren't broken to harness, but they were fresh and strong, and once they got it into their heads that they had to run, they ran. Ruff was straining forward, staring at the dark world, aware of something nagging at his mind, some omen or promise or dread—it hit him.

It was dawn. The sky was graying in the east. He swore bitterly. They were miles from Lincoln, but now Cash nodded south and east. The broad, dark band of the Missouri River was visible, barely visible, and abutting it the low dark jumble of Bismarck.

"There it is!" Cash called out. He could make out the fort itself now, and so could Ruff, as the skies brightened and a narrow orange-gold band of light spread out across the sky like dawn fire.

Cash went to the whip again. Ruff found himself biting at his lip. It was dawn—the dying time. He wondered briefly, irrelevantly, why they didn't execute men at sunset with the day dying, the world growing dark. No, they had to see the bright promise of a new day, the color and grandeur of morning, and know they would never see another.

"Lay that lash on them, Cash!" Ruff shouted, though he knew the instructions were useless. But you had to do something—and when there was nothing to do, you ranted and cursed as Justice did now.

There was a thin line of the purest beaten gold along

the dark horizon. The off-horse faltered and Cash yanked his head up with the reins.

Bismarck was suddenly there, and then the fort, too far ahead; and from the fort Ruff heard, or imagined he heard, the shouts of command, the firing squad being assembled, the prisoner being led forth . . .

"No shots yet," Cash said. His face was twisted with emotion, his lip turned back, his eyes red and haunted. Ruff wondered what his own face looked like.

The front gate was just being opened as they reached it. There was a challenge from the sentry, but they ignored it, rumbling through in a maelstrom of dust.

"There!" Cash shouted, and Ruff saw it too. The kid with a dark cloth sack over his head being tied to the wooden post, the soldiers lined up, rifles in hand, awaiting the order of the colonel, who stood by, bitter and rigid. The woman had collapsed in Sergeant Mack Pierce's massive arms.

Heads turned and someone cried out. Cash Williams drove the stagecoach directly between the firing squad and the post, wrenching back hard on the reins, jerking the horses' heads back, froth flying from their mouths, sweat staining their dark hides.

Colonel MacEnroe was already there, ready to chew out the crazy civilian stage driver who had intruded on this tense moment, but he saw the man in buckskins jump down from the box and walk toward him and he watched with curious, half-hopeful eyes.

"Call 'em off, sir," Ruff Justice said. "Billy Sondberg's an innocent man and we've got the proof in the coach."

Mary Sondberg was looking up now, her broad, honest face chalky, tear-streaked. She made a small, gasping noise and cried out with joy. "True?" she asked, taking a step forward.

"Yes, it's true," Ruff answered.

"Ruffin," the colonel began, "I hope this is no trick, I just hope that."

162

"It's straight, sir." The coach had settled in its own dust now. Cash Williams was down beside the horses. The door to the coach swung open and the two women emerged. Carrie cried out and on weak legs went to where Billy, the sack still over his head, waited at the post. She clung to him, sobbing from way down deep.

Ruth Dawkens walked to where Ruff Justice stood and she whispered, "Tall man, you cut it close."

"What sort of proof have you got, Ruff?" the colonel asked, wanting, but not quite being able, to believe that Sondberg had been cleared.

Justice walked him to the open coach. Lieutenant Ed Sharpe, trussed still, his eyes flaming with anger, lay looking up from the floor.

"It was Sharpe."

"Lieutenant Sharpe killed the girl?"

"Afraid so, sir." Colonel MacEnroe was an old-line officer who nurtured the idea that all officers were gentlemen, and if they weren't, they deserved to be shot.

This one would be.

"He confessed in front of me, Cash Williams, and the two women. If that's not enough witnesses, there are a dozen more in Bear Creek or en route, including the dead girl's father."

"Sharpe . . .?" MacEnroe shook his head. "Sergeant Pierce! Get this man out of this coach and escort him to the stockade. Release the prisoner."

Carrie Dean cried out with delight. Sondberg's legs were wobbling a little as the black sack mask was removed. The soldiers in the firing squad relaxed, putting their rifles down. Except for one.

The soldier deliberately lifted his rifle and aimed it. Ruff Justice had his Colt in his hand and he fired four times from the waist. The soldier jerked around and was blown backward, to lie twitching against the ground in a smear of gore and dust.

MacEnroe roared with anger and ripped the gun from Justice's hand. "Damn you, damn you, Ruffin! Are you mad?"

Ruff just stood there, shaking his head once. The corporal of the guard was hunched over the soldier Ruff had shot. He stood, his hands spread.

"Dead, sir. Mister Justice has killed him . . . but he ain't no soldier. I never seen this man before in my life."

But then the soldier had never had occasion to meet Charity Blaine.

16

The colonel was in an expansive mood. He had his desk-drawer bottle of whiskey in front of him, and the two drinks he had already downed had given his face a cheerful reddish tint.

Mary Sondberg continued to quietly sob tears of joy in the corner. Mack Pierce stood by her with a quiet pride in his eyes. Billy Sondberg repeated over and over, "I can't believe it, I just can't believe it. I knew I was a goner. I can't believe it."

"Why, you damned fool," Mack Pierce said with tenderness, "it's a wonder you're not dead, and you would of had no one to blame but yourself, Billy Sondberg."

"I know it," the kid sighed. He was shaken. The colonel was enough of an aristocrat not to want to drink with enlisted men, but he broke his rule on this occasion and offered a glass of whiskey to the kid. Ruff didn't think Billy Sondberg had ever tried the stuff before, but he couldn't refuse it, and he needed the steadying.

"I don't understand why you didn't just admit that you were walking out with Carrie here at the time of the murder," Mary Sondberg said.

"He was absent from his post, Mrs. Sondberg," the colonel said. "Something he will still have to do punishment for."

"But when it was a choice between that punishment and being shot for murder!"

"It would have gone hard on Carrie," Ruff said. "You wouldn't know if you don't know Dan Dean."

"No father would actually harm his daughter for that," Mary objected, showing how tenderhearted she actually was.

"They have, they do."

"It was all my fault," Carrie said. "I should have come forward. I don't know why I didn't."

Ruth Dawkens reminded her, "You had given your word, Carrie."

"Yes, but there has to be a time to use common sense and not follow an oath blindly. What sort of life would I have had without Billy, knowing I had allowed him to be shot? Why, it was foolish—and if it hadn't been for Mister Justice . . ."

"Mister Justice seems frequently to be in the right place when needed," Colonel MacEnroe said with proprietary pride, forgetting he had been ready to tie Ruff up to that splintered post and cut the firing squad loose on him.

"How did you know that man wasn't a soldier, Ruff?"

"I recognized Blaine, but what drew my eye was the fact that he wasn't wearing a black armband—he must not have been able to rustle one up quick enough."

"How could he have hoped to get away with that?" Ruth asked.

"He could have done so very easily," Justice said. "Up until the last second he thought, everyone thought, that the firing squad was going to do the work. I guess you know that it's traditional for there to be only one live round in those rifles so that all the men don't carry the burden of guilt—they can kid themselves that they were firing blanks. Well, Charity wasn't firing a blank."

"But if the colonel had called off the execution, given Billy a stay?"

"That wouldn't have stopped Charity Blaine. There are a dozen simple ways to get a man in a cell. Charity probably knew some that wouldn't occur to us readily. No, he had been paid and primed. Blaine had a sort of pride that made him obsessively determined to do that job, to have something to brag about maybe. Anyway, he's gone and it makes the air in Dakota a little cleaner."

"Ed Sharpe has admitted everything for the record. He was nearly blasé about it. He's convinced himself that it was Katie Maxwell's fault. He'll be court-martialed next week." The colonel shook his head. "Things got tangled up, didn't they, Ruffin?"

"They did that, sir. We owe the Great Western stage line some money, by the way."

The colonel frowned, but he said to Mack Pierce, "Company fund handle that, Mack?"

"Yes, sir."

"What about Fox Fight, Ruff? Is he gone or not?"

"No idea. I hope so. I think he's just a man out of place and time. He would have been a hero twenty years ago, a warrior and leader. Now he's a renegade."

The colonel winced a little. He didn't like the reservation system any more than Justice did, but he was sworn to enforce the rules.

"I'm sorry about your sister, Miss Dawkens," MacEnroe said, changing the subject. "If you like we can send the word out that—"

"Leave her be," Ruth answered. "At first I thought it was an incredibly rash thing for Marcia to do. Rash and bizarre. Now I don't know. After thinking about it, I've come to agree with Mister Justice. She didn't fit our world, my world. There was a savage streak in my sister, and more important, a need to be loved, which no man in this world seemed to be able to satisfy. They found her unappealing because she was different. Fox Fight found her attractive because she is different. Maybe their lives won't be comfortable or even long . . . but they'll have each other for a time."

"Yes." MacEnroe grew thoughtful and Ruff thought he spied the tip of a romantic iceberg in the colonel's eyes. He asked Justice, "You'll be taking some time off, will you?"

"A little. Until my leg's healed up properly. I'll have to know when the wedding is so I can get back for that. Or was that going to be today?"

Carrie Dean turned a deep red-violet. Billy Sondberg blushed as well.

"I've got some punishment time coming, Mister Justice," the kid said.

"I'm aware of that. I thought maybe Colonel MacEnroe would give some consideration to the anguish you've already had, the time you've already spent in the stockade." Ruff looked at the colonel, who had that boxed-in expression as Ruff, the young couple, and an anxious Mary Sondberg all watched him hopefully.

"Private Sondberg was absent from his post," the colonel said.

"Yes, sir."

"I can't let that go unpunished."

"No, sir."

"What time is it?" MacEnroe asked obliquely.

Mack Pierce glanced at his watch. "Ten o'clock, sir."

"Very well. Return this man to the stockade." Carrie Dean's face fell. "I want him to serve an additional hour's punishment. And find that chaplain, Mack. Tell him we've got a wedding at eleven o'clock."

They had themselves a wedding. For a time Ruff thought Mack Pierce, who had broken out in a cold sweat, was going to make it a double, but he fought off the impulse. Ruff, still in his torn buckskins, stood by with Ruth Dawkens. Mack was best man, and the colonel gave the bride away.

"Mack," the colonel told his first sergeant when the ceremony was over, "we haven't given the young couple a wedding present. Make out a two-week pass for Private Sondberg. I'm not having any trooper of mine married without benefit of a honeymoon."

"Yes, sir," Mack said with an enthusiastic salute.

"I'm getting soft," MacEnroe said to Justice.

"Really?" Justice raised an eyebrow. "All right for me to begin my sick leave, sir?"

"Yes, of course," the colonel answered.

Ruff Justice already had started toward the door. His arm was around Ruth Dawkens. Ruff just barely heard the colonel mutter, "I wish I was that sick."

The hotel room had a window that faced the west and Ruff Justice could lie in bed and watch as sunset sprawled across the late skies, staining it in intricate, changing patterns.

He liked the view, he liked it very much. But he had no objections when Ruth Dawkens walked in front of the window, naked, sleek, her blond hair down across her shoulders. She lifted her arms and stretched, and her breasts lifted, her waist extended itself as she cut a silhouette against the sunset, a silhouette no artist would dream of attempting.

She turned and, hands on hips, legs spread, faced him challengingly.

"Well?"

"Well?"

"Do you still like it? Do you like the way I look, the way I move?"

"Woman, I like everything about you, but I'm getting tired now of liking it at a distance."

He patted the bed beside him and Ruth walked across

the room, her breasts moving, jouncing with primitive rhythm, her stride completely feline.

She sat down and then rolled to Ruff, her lips parting to meet his, her hands going to his shoulders as he wrapped her in his arms. Her flesh was warm and smooth against his. He caught the faint scent of lilac about her, the slight musk of her body that revealed an eagerness, a need. She was lithe and warm, tender and demanding alternately. She was good to be with, and when she strove for her own needed release, she found it quickly, ably, and enjoyed it to the limit.

Now she straddled Ruff and raised herself, reaching between her legs to find his solid shaft. She gave a little grunt of pleasure and lifted herself, positioning him as she settled, a distant light shining in her eyes. Ruff took her by the back of the neck and pulled her down, his mouth smothering hers as her hips began to sway and roll, her downy pelvis to nudge his with insistent prompting.

"Can you feel that?" she asked his ear. Her teeth teased the lobe of it. "Leaking from me. So warm. All your doing, tall man. Don't move. That's just right, Mister Justice."

Ruff let his hands roam up her sleek thighs, cup her breasts, his thumbs toying with the taut pink nipples. Then he reached between her legs, touching her where he entered her. Ruth's own fingers came to meet his, intertwining with his as she sat upright, her head thrown back, her lips parted as her body worked against Ruff's, as she pressed herself against her own fingers and Ruff's urging hands until with a shudder she came, falling forward to lie against him, her heated body trembling, shaken.

And then Ruff began to search for his own release, to arch his back and lift her as she softly murmured. He rolled her over then, holding her warm thighs so that she couldn't slip away, and he pinned her to the bed, her legs lifting high into the air as he slipped his hands beneath her buttocks and hoisted her to meet him. He drove into her and Ruth's searching fingers touched his shaft as he did so, urging him on until with a violent thrust and a vast shudder he reached his own hard completion.

They lay together talking of Marcia, of the wedding, of Bear Creek and Updike and the army life and of everything and nothing. Her fingers traced the whorl of his ear, toyed with the dark hair on his chest, found his lips, and returned to settle between his legs where still the slow, hard pulsing of blood kept him a solid presence between her thighs.

"Hungry," she yawned hours later. "I'm really hungry, Mister Justice."

"What time is it?"

"I don't know. Midnight, dawn? Not noon. Sun's not up."

"It's early enough to eat, I think. Want to go out?"

"Rather have 'em bring it here," she said in a distant, childlike voice.

"Yes, well, they don't do that at this hotel, darling."

"You've probably tried it," she said with what might have been a hint of jealousy in her tone.

"No," Ruff lied. He was rubbing her lovely bottom, his finger trailing lazily up the warm cleft. She shuddered each time it reached the tip of her tailbone.

"Again?" she asked, and she began to sway against him once more.

"Now you've got me thinking about food."

"Steak."

"Steak and eggs."

"With potatoes."

"Oh, woman, you'll pay the price when you're older."

"I'm not older. I work it off, don't I?"

"You do do that."

"Steak and eggs then," Ruth sulked. "And potatoes—and apple pie."

"And a bowl of cream."

She giggled politely and poked a finger into Ruff's ribs. He rolled away and lay looking at the dark ceiling. Somewhere distantly a cowboy yelled.

"Well?"

"Well what?" Ruff Justice asked.

"Do we eat or do we make love?"

"At the same time?" he suggested.

"That would be all right too. But as you've pointed out, it's one or the other."

"Life is cruel," Ruff Justice speculated. Finally, however, he rose from the bed, and Ruth murmured a complaint as she was denied his nearness.

"Life is cruel," she agreed.

Ruff bent low, kissed her breasts, her throat, her lips, and then pulled her to a sitting position. "Dress. We'll eat quickly."

"Good thinking," Ruth Dawkens answered. She rose and dressed—quickly. Her hair was pinned up in short order, her little hat positioned on her blond head. Ruff, who had brought along his dark town suit and white shirt, was just now straightening his own hat, a fawn-colored stetson with a narrow black band.

"Ready?" She was bright and eager, sated with lovemaking, beautiful. Ruff just watched her eyes, the smile playing about her lips for a minute before he answered.

"All ready. My arm."

He gave her his elbow and she took it with both her hands. Together then they went out into the corridor and down the stairs into the lobby. The hotel restaurant was closed and so they went out onto the boardwalk. It would have to be the Butter & Eggs down the block.

"Do you think it's open?" Ruth asked, squinting down the dark street toward the restaurant.

"If it's not, we'll open it. I've got food on my mind now."

Ruff took a step forward and then the rifle rang out from across the street. Ruth Dawkens went down in a heap, blood streaming across her face.

17

When he heard the rifle shot, Ruff instinctively pitched to one side, drawing his Colt pistol from its shoulder holster. He saw the muzzle flash from the second shot, heard the bullet bury itself in the wooden wall of the hotel, and then saw Ruth lying still and bloody nearby.

Oh, God, not again. Ruff rolled toward her, his heart beating rapidly. His eyes were on the rooftop opposite, but his fingers searched her face, her throat, desperately needing to discover breath, a pulse.

It couldn't end like the last time, with Louise lying dead and bloody against the earth, the pines darkening her pale face . . .

The front door of the hotel had burst open. A lantern flashed in Ruff's eyes. Two men with rifles stood there, peering across the street into the darkness. A small man with a white mustache and round, pink cheeks appeared. Ruff realized he must be the doctor. He looked Ruth over, his small mouth pursed and concerned.

"Well? What is it? You can't let her die," Ruff Justice said, and he realized that he had hold of the doctor's lapels, shaking him.

"Easy. Take it easy. She's all right, mister."

"Who the hell was it?" someone asked. "Who would do a thing like that?"

But Justice already knew and he was sprinting across the street, Colt in hand, leaving the questioning voices, the pale lamplit faces behind as he raced to cut off Tandy Monroe.

"Where you going?" a fading voice called, and then Ruff was into the alley beside the dry-goods store, down it, and to the wooden stairs that led to the rooftops. Tandy would have used these stairs to get on the roof in the first place. Ruff hesitated a split second, peering upward at the dark line of the roof against the starry background.

He saw no rifle barrel, no hat, and so he went up— fast, four or five steps at a time, the little Colt New Line in his hand. He reached the roof and was driven back over the side by three rapidly fired shots.

"Smart, Tandy," Ruff muttered as he remained hunched against the weathered wood of the platform. Instead of running, Tandy had remained where he was, waiting to blow the head off the first man who poked his nose up, knowing the first man would be Ruff Justice.

"Tandy!"

There was no answer, although Monroe wouldn't have given anything away. Ruff knew where he was, knew who it was. Tandy was in a bad spot, but then he was a desperate man right now. The word was already around about Tandy. He would never work again. There was nothing for him to do but go into the wilderness and try to live out his years alone. Maybe that was what he planned to do.

After he got his revenge on Ruff Justice.

"Tandy!" This time Ruff moved as he spoke, rolling up onto the rooftop, which was tar paper over pine planks. Tandy's rifle fired twice more, but Justice had kept moving, rolling behind the chimney he had spotted his first time up.

A bullet sang off the base of the chimney, scattering brick dust to the light wind.

Then it was still again. The stars yawned in the deep, soft sky. Somewhere distantly Ruff could hear crowd noises, confused muttering, empty bravado.

The footsteps raced away from Ruff and he sprang from behind the chimney, following the running silhouette with the sights of the New Line. He squeezed off and heard a yelp of pain. The silhouetted figure went off balance for a stride, half-turned, and then flew through space, leaping toward the opposite rooftop.

It hadn't been much of a hit, but maybe it would slow Tandy down. Justice shed his coat and sprinted across the roof himself. Across the alley the slightly lower roof of the Bismarck bank showed, geometrical, dark, seemingly flimsy. Ruff leapt and Tandy's rifle fired again.

That one wasn't close.

Ruff hit the rooftop harder than he had expected. His knees were driven up and the wind was knocked out of his lungs temporarily. He lay on his belly, watching the darkness.

"Tandy, give it up."

Tandy wouldn't answer. He had all the advantages, especially in firepower. Monroe carried that needle gun with a seventeen-shot capacity. But it didn't matter.

Ruff was going to nail the man. Finally nail him cold.

Tandy had come hunting, sniping, trying to kill from cover instead of standing up and having at it. He had missed Ruff and gotten Ruth. He might have killed her. The doctor said she was all right, but head wounds are funny things. He knew a trooper who had shrugged off a crease on the skull, laughing over it, and two weeks later suddenly keeled over dead.

"Tandy!"

Rifle shots answered the yell and Justice returned a

shot at the muzzle flashes. He heard his bullet sing off metal, heard Tandy scream.

"My thumb. You shot my thumb off!"

The rifle clattered to the roof. Monroe was up now, running again, holding his injured hand. Ruff was on his heels, seeing the rifle with the splintered stock and the drops of maroon blood.

Tandy was climbing down the wooden ladder attached to the side of the building. Ruff leaned out, sighted, and then lost Tandy to the shadows. He started down himself, teeth tightly clenched, his muscles aching with the tension.

Tandy was into the muddy alley behind the bank, stumbling as he ran. Justice ducked as a shot from Tandy's handgun flew past his head.

Then Tandy was gone again, the alley empty.

The big Dakota Stable was in front of Ruff—a three-story tall barn with a huge hayloft where winter feed for half the town's horses was kept. Ruff looked up at the outer door to the loft. A hay hook dangled from the tackle outside and above the high loading door.

Justice shoved his gun behind his belt and started up, hand over hand.

He reached the loft in less than a minute with burning hands and a racing heart. He ducked under the lintel and entered the cool, hay- and horse-smelling interior of the Dakota.

He crouched, listening, his eyes seeing nothing for a long minute. Tandy should have been down below. Trying for his horse? Possibly, although Ruff doubted Monroe, on the run, would have stabled his horse here. Any horse, then—he wanted any horse.

Maybe. Justice listened to the scrabbling sounds of mice in the loft, the shifting of the horses' feet, the creaking of the wooden building. On cat's feet he inched forward in a crouch, one hand on the loft rail, the other filled with the cool steel of his revolver. He peered up and over the rail, seeing nothing.

He worked his way toward the stairs at the far end of the loft, moving carefully, placing each foot gingerly. The cry from below split the air. Ruff heard it, saw the horse bolt for the door of the Dakota, saw the buckskinned leg slung over the horse's back. He started to fire and held back, cursing.

He leapt for the stairs and was down them in seconds. The first horse he saw was a palomino. Whose it was he didn't know, and he didn't care. He was up over the animal's flanks, digging boot heels in. The palomino half-reared and then beelined it up the alley. In the distance Ruff could just barely make out the dark form of a running horse.

He leaned low over the withers and held on, his hand knotted into the white mane of the borrowed palomino.

The plains were empty, dark, endless. Someone had trained that palomino right and it minded the guiding pressure of Ruff's knees as well as a lot of horses minded a hard bit.

Tandy seemed to be losing ground, but Ruff wasn't sure. The palomino was plenty of horse, however. The chase took on an air of unreality. There was only the effortful running of the long-striding horse, its mane swirling, its eyes wide, the moving pale muscle between Ruff's legs, the soft thudding of hooves against the prairie earth.

Tandy disappeared.

He was there and then he wasn't, and Justice knew instantly what had happened, or thought he did. There had to be a coulee up ahead, a dry wash that was impossible to see until you were upon it.

He slowed the palomino a little and then picked out the rim of the coulee against the surrounding darkness.

Tandy was going to make a battle of it. He was through running.

Ruff saw the dark figure to his right and his Colt came up automatically. It was only a sorrel horse, its sides flecked with foam, hobbling toward them.

Tandy was afoot down in the coulee. Ruff grinned at the darkness. He grinned, and there wasn't a bit of humor in it. Tandy had wanted to move soundlessly, to slip away through the brush in the coulee bottom. Monroe was never that good an Indian. He had forgotten who he was up against.

"I got you, Monroe. I got you now, my friend."

Justice slid from the palomino's back and scurried to the edge of the coulee. He crouched there, listening, eyes probing the darkness. Left or right? Which way had Tandy gone? He was lying still down there now, knowing that his best defense.

Ruff waited, sitting on his heels, his pistol in his hand. He had all night.

The moon slowly rose at Ruff's back, a great near-orange ball as it peered over the horizon. He moved carefully along the coulee, looking for tracks by moonlight.

He didn't much like the idea of going into the brush after a wounded animal, but that was the way it had to be. He found the place where the sandy edge of the bluff had been broken down by hasty boots.

"Ready, Tandy?" Justice asked aloud. There was no answer, not a whisper of sound, no sudden gunshot. Was there a chance Tandy had been hit harder than Ruff thought? Maybe the bullet that had smashed his rifle stock and relieved him of his right thumb had passed into his body.

It was possible. Monroe might be out there dead or bleeding to death. It was a lot more likely he was playing possum.

Ruff slid down the bluff in a shower of sand and

crept forward, eyes on the ground where the deep, indistinct tracks were carved, on the dark, tangled brush ahead of him: willow and sumac, sage and greasewood twisted into a dense thicket. Except Ruff hadn't heard a lot of noise when Tandy was seeking a hiding place. He hadn't gotten into the heavy brush; he was looking for a trail through the brush.

The moon had gotten smaller, silver-blue, harder. It peered into the gulley as Ruff moved forward.

Tandy popped up in front of him from out of the sand and his gun exploded in his fist. He yelled something indistinct, venomous, at Ruff. His face was weirdly lighted by the muzzle flash. The bullet flew past Justice's head as Ruff flung himself to one side, firing back.

Tandy's gunsights followed him, the Remington .44 in his hand blasting away. Justice fired back one more time and saw Tandy half-turn. Then the man started running for the brush, holding his side.

Justice was on his feet, racing after him, and he threw himself through the air in a long dive, taking Tandy down.

"Damn you, damn you! Kill you, you son of a bitch," Tandy screamed. He kicked out savagely, thrust his pistol into Ruff's face, and squeezed off. The hammer fell on an empty chamber and Ruff clubbed him on the side of his head with his own pistol.

Tandy sat halfway up and looked at Justice with eyes that reflected the round silver-blue moon. Then he flopped back, unconscious.

"Tandy, so help me I've never hated any man as much as I do you." The temptation was great to finish him off. That was what he deserved. But the anger had cooled in Ruff's heart. He wanted only to be done with Tandy Monroe, but not to kill him.

He wanted to get to Bismarck and fast, to see for himself that Ruth was all right.

Ruff threw Tandy over his shoulder and started up the sandy bank.

"You bastard, Justice!" Tandy screamed. Playing possum. He ya**d the bowie from Ruff's belt and slashed out at Ruff with it. Justice flung himself to one side and both men rolled down the sandy bluff in a storm of dust.

At the bottom Tandy was on his feet first, circling Ruff, the bowie in his left hand. The right hand still dripped dark blood.

Justice backed away, his hand going once to his empty holster. He had lost the Colt in the spill.

Tandy smiled nastily. "Now you gonna die, Ruffin! Finally."

"What happened, Tandy? What made you turn like this? Was the money that important? You killed scores of people, let them be killed . . ."

The talking didn't distract Tandy any. He continued to wave that big bowie before Ruff's eyes.

Justice needed a little distance, a little time. He backed away, still talking to Tandy. "You shot that woman, Tandy. She did nothing to you. None of those you killed did anything to you."

Justice took the chance. The skinning knife was still in his boot, with its narrow and murderously sharp blade. He crouched and came up with it, throwing it underhand as Tandy started forward with a roar of anger.

The knife caught Tandy Monroe at the base of the throat, going in to the haft. The bowie was raised high and now it fell harmlessly past Ruff's eyes as Tandy crumpled up and fell facefirst into the sand.

Ruff Justice backed up a step and then sat down, his long arms looped around his knees. He looked at the silver moon and at the silver bowie lying against the sand, at the dark stain seeping into the sand.

Then, with a heavy sigh, Justice got up, recovered his

weapons, and went looking for a horse. He threw Tandy over the gimpy sorrel and started back toward Bismarck. It was a long ride, but Tandy didn't mind it.

She was propped up in bed. Sunlight streamed through the white lace curtains of the hotel room. They'd wrapped a bandage around her head, but it didn't do a thing to mar Ruth Dawkens' attractiveness.

Ruff sat on the windowsill looking out at the sunny street. A single wagon rolled out of town toward the lazy blue Missouri.

"Some sick leave for you, taking care of me," Ruth said.

"It's been fun," Ruff answered, turning toward her. He rose and crossed to the bed.

"Fun? Taking care of a sick woman?"

He touched her pale hair and smiled. Lifting her hand, he kissed it. "Yes. Fun. Good. Good to see you heal and grow strong—"

"And not die." Ruth watched him tenderly.

"Yes. That's it."

"You've seen a lot of dying, haven't you, Ruff Justice?"

"I've seen it. I've caused it. That's what I mean—to feed you, to see that you're warm, to watch you heal . . . I feel damn near godlike. It's a good feeling to see you lying here, knowing that your needs are taken care of."

"Most all of them," she said with a sly smile.

"What else could you need, woman?"

"I've got a soul as well as a body, Mister Justice." Ruth turned back the sheet and lay there looking up invitingly, and Ruff Justice crawled in beside her to heal the woman, body and soul.

WESTWARD HO!

The following is the opening chapter from the next novel in the gun-blazing, action-packed new Ruff Justice series from Signet:

Ruff Justice #18: THE RIVERBOAT QUEEN

She could have been a dancer. She had the moves, the grace, the physical determination, the raw beauty. But it was fortunate for Ruff Justice that she wasn't any dancer. All of that splendid natural talent had been put to other uses, and Ruth Dawkens was really quite good at what she did.

She sat facing him, straddling his hips, her long blond hair cascading across her pale, smooth shoulders in a silvery torrent. Her breasts were full, high, pink-budded, smooth beneath the hands of Ruffin T. Justice, the civilian scout working under Colonel MacEnroe at Fort Lincoln, Dakota Territory.

Justice was no dancer either. It would have been a waste of time to try to teach him, but he too, it seemed, had his raw physical talent. At least Ruth Dawkens thought so, and no one had proved her a liar.

The woman with the warmly lighted eyes bent low and kissed Ruff Justice on the lips and eyes before sitting up again, letting her finger trail along the line of his long dark mustache, which drooped past his jawline, framing a slightly mocking mouth.

"I wish I didn't have to leave," Ruth said.

"You don't." Ruff's hands reached behind the woman and gripped her smooth, ivory-white buttocks, feeling the strength beneath the soft, feminine layer of flesh.

She quivered slightly and smiled. "Yes, I do, Ruff. There's nothing for me here, and you know it."

"There's me."

She made a small contented sound and leaned forward to kiss him again. "I know that, but you'll be going back to work soon too. The colonel isn't going to want this sick leave going on forever."

"No." Ruff frowned slightly at the thought of MacEnroe.

"Since there's never been any word about Marcia . . ." She fell silent, thinking about her sister, her lost sister who had run off with a renegade Indian. "Well" —she shrugged—"we knew it had to end."

"Not today," he said, his hands running up her arms to her shoulders.

"No, not today." She lay against him and her hips lifted and rolled to one side slightly, a small movement that inflamed Ruff Justice. His fingers trailed down the knuckles of her spine to the cleft of her ass. She sighed contentedly and snuggled against him, her pelvis nudging his, rising and falling.

Ruff felt her hand reach back and find him, her fingers encouraged him, stroking, gripping fingers, grown familiar now, competent, and eager—a dancer's fingers.

"I don't want to go," she said. Her words were muffled. She spoke against his chest, her dancer's body beginning to speed its rhythm, its thrust, as her inner muscles worked against Justice.

"I know."

"Don't want to," she puffed, "but I have to."

Ruth sat up and leaned her head back, her lips parted, her eyes half-closed as she slowly raised and lowered herself on Ruff's shaft. Justice watched her, liking the concentration on her face, the distant pleasure in her eyes, the cascade of silver hair, the rising and falling breasts, ripe and round, the patch of soft down, the heat of her body, the sleek strength of her thighs, the length of her calves rounded with firm muscle, the small feet.

She lifted herself higher yet and then settled with a deep sigh, finishing with a series of tiny, jerking movements, her body growing wet, heavy, as she sagged forward unsteadily against Ruff, who had found his own rhythm and now lifted her with the action of his body, spreading her wider with his searching fingers, hearing her breathing in his ear, the urging, meaningless little words before he spilled himself in Ruth and lay back to clutch at her, to touch and fondle, to feel her sweet breath and searching lips on his face, throat, and chest.

The door banged open and the woman just barged in.

She was tall and angular and raucous, with a blue peacoat on her back, a mop of sawed-off red hair spilling out from under a sea captain's hat.

"Just about what I figured—I know men!" she said.

"Good," Ruff Justice said mildly. "Then you know what I'm going to do to you if you don't turn around and get out of here, woman."

"All talk. Just like 'em all. Get up, boy. You are Ruffin T. Justice, aren't you? Your colonel's got a job for you. Namely, working for me."

"Colonel MacEnroe sent you here," Ruff sputtered a

little. He and the colonel had their share of run-ins, but this didn't seem like MacEnroe's tactics.

"Ah, hell, no. He gave me some malarkey about you being on sick leave or some such. I said to myself, If he's like any man I ever knew, he's sick with a blonde beside him."

Ruff sat up slowly, Ruth rolling to one side to draw her knees up and tug the sheet up under her chin. They could only stare at the big redheaded woman. Big she was, but not fat, and not so old as Ruff had first imagined. Middle twenties, perhaps.

"Well, let's get up. I told the colonel I couldn't hardly get my work done while the man who was *supposedly* going to help me was frolickin' in the sack."

"Look, Miss . . ."

"Shore. I'm Sally Shore, you probably heard of me, everyone has."

Ruff hadn't, but she didn't give him time to say so. She went on, "The colonel wouldn't tell me where you were, so I stormed out of there. It didn't take much to find this cozy port, though. A hotel, I figured, then I give the desk clerk a spot of silver money and he sent me up." She had her hands on her hips. "So, here I am, there you are. Get up and let's get together!"

For a minute Ruff thought she was going to reach down and flip the sheet back, but she restrained herself. He took a deep breath before he let himself respond.

"Sally Shore, I want you to turn around and get out of here. I mean, right now. I don't know what your business is and I don't care."

"The army—"

"The army's given me some time off. When they need me back, they'll let me know in some slightly more discreet manner. I don't know if you're dumb or just all brass, but I'd appreciate it if you'd back into the hall and think it over."

Sally Shore just stared at him, her tongue pushing at the inside of her cheek. She winked.

She just winked, turned around, and with her hands thrust in her coat pockets, she sauntered out into the hallway, closing the door sharply behind her.

"What," Ruth said laughing, "was that?"

Justice had no answer for her. It beat all. The woman was plain audacious. Ruff got up. He sat on the edge of the bed rubbing his head for a minute.

"What are you going to do?" Ruth asked, her hand on his back.

"See what she wants. If I don't, she'll be back."

From the hallway Sally Shore called out, "You're damned right I'll be back, Ruffin T. Justice!"

Ruth laughed. Ruff shook his head and got up from the bed, crossing the room to where his clothes lay on the chair—his buckskin pants and buckskin shirt, white hat. His gun belt rested on one post of the chair.

Ruth, yawning, also rose.

"I thought maybe you'd wait here," Ruff said.

"Can't, Mister Justice." She put her arms around his waist, rested her head on his chest. "I've got to see about a ticket east."

"You're seriously going?" He tilted her chin up.

"I'm seriously going," she said. There was just a little moisture gathering in the corners of her deep-brown eyes. Ruff kissed the top of her head.

"I'll be back later. We'll make it a fine good-bye," he promised. He had started toward the door before she replied.

"All right. Ruffin . . ."

He looked back expectantly, but she just shook her head and turned away. Ruff stood silently for a moment, watching her bare back. Then he went out to deal with Sally Shore.

She was leaning against the wall in the corridor, one foot propped up behind her. Her hat was tilted rakishly on her dark-red hair.

"Through? I thought maybe you'd pause for another helping."

"What do you want?" Justice asked. He hadn't quite warmed to the woman and she wasn't helping matters any.

"Told you what I wanted. Colonel says you're my helper. Let's get going."

"Lady, you're just a little pushy."

"Yeah, I know. That's what got me where I am." She came away from the wall. "You ready?"

"No. I have to talk to the colonel before I do anything."

"Just red tape. I'll tell you all you need to know."

Justice wasn't listening. He was walking down the corridor toward the hotel stairs, wondering how a day that began so promisingly could have turned sour so quickly.

He managed to recover his horse from the stable and ride out of Bismarck toward the fort without Sally Shore on his tail, but he met her again inside the colonel's office. She wasn't going to be that easy to shake, it seemed.

"Hello, Ruff," Colonel MacEnroe said from behind his desk. He was a hard man with clean features, a silver mustache, and the air of authority. Just now he looked a little bedazzled. "You've met Miss Shore?"

"Yes," Justice said. He took a corner chair and sat down, crossing his long legs, balancing his hat on his knee. Sally Shore yawned broadly.

"Sorry, Ruff. How's the leg by the way?" Justice had

been nicked by a bullet, the cause of the sick leave that Sally Shore had so rudely and abruptly ended.

"It's fine now, sir."

"Apparently the man's in working order from one end to the other," Sally Shore said. "So let's skip that, and skip 'How's your ma and how's your pa' and get down to brass tacks."

MacEnroe's face paled just a little and the muscles at the hinge of his jaw twitched, but he didn't respond. Instead, he turned to Justice.

"As you know, Ruffin, the Sioux are kicking up their heels to the northwest. We're having a hell of a time supplying Fort Benton overland. The freighters won't even try it anymore. Miss Shore is going to have at it."

"She's a teamster?"

"Steamboat captain." The colonel held up his hand as Ruff started to object automatically. "I know, I know— it's a bad stretch of water from here to the Marias. Shallow some places, quick in others. No steam boat has ever tried to get that far up the Missou i, bu Miss Shore has a shallow draft vessel that she is so ivinced can make it through to Benton, and, Justic . we have to take the chance. Regiment has made the lecision already."

"The Sioux will never let her get throug.. Aside from that, Jack Troll and his thugs cont ol the river from here to Fort Union. Benton is four hund ed land miles from Lincoln, the river route makes it half again as long."

"I know that, Ruff," the colonel said, "but the men at Benton need food, ammunition, tools, to complete that fort by winter. They're virtually cut off, besieged by the Sioux. This is a long chance, but it's about the only one we have."

Ruff Justice felt his mouth tighten. He didn't like any

part of this idea. If Regiment didn't know the upper Missouri, he did. It was a wild, unpredictable thing. He had rapids and falls and hostile Indians ahead of him, river bandits and hard weather.

And, worst of all, he had Miss Sally Shore to deal with. He looked again at the smug, overconfident red-headed woman and then shrugged.

"All right. I'll have at it, colonel. All I need is a little time for a few good-byes."

JOIN THE *RUFF JUSTICE* READERS' PANEL

Help us bring you more of the books you like by filling out this survey and mailing it in today.

1 Book Title: _____

  Book #: _____

2. Using the scale below, how would you rate this book on the following features? Please write in one rating from 0-10 for each feature in the spaces provided.

POOR	NOT SO GOOD		O.K.			GOOD		EXCEL-LENT	
0	1	2	3	4	5	6	7	8	9	10

RATING

Overall opinion of book .... _____
Plot/Story .... _____
Setting/Location .... _____
Writing Style .... _____
Character Development .... _____
Conclusion/Ending .... _____
Scene on Front Cover .... _____

3. About how many western books do you buy for yourself each month? _____

4. How would you classify yourself as a reader of westerns? I am a ( ) light ( ) medium ( ) heavy reader.

5. What is your education?
  ( ) High School (or less) ( ) 4 yrs. college
  ( ) 2 yrs. college   ( ) Post Graduate

6. Age _____ 7. Sex: ( ) Male ( ) Female

Please Print Name_____

Address_____

City _____ State _____ Zip _____

Phone # ( )_____

Thank you. Please send to New American Library, Research Dept., 1633 Broadway, New York, NY 10019.

SIGNET Westerns You'll Enjoy by Leo P. Kelley

(0451)